JOURNEY TO **STAR WARS**: THE FORCE AWAKENS

THE WEAPON OF A JEDI

A LUKE SKYWALKER ADVENTURE

WRITTEN BY
JASON FRY

ILLUSTRATED BY
PHIL NOTO

EGMONT

We bring stories to life

First published in Great Britain 2015
by Egmont UK Limited, The Yellow Building,
1 Nicholas Road, London W11 4AN

© and ™ 2015 Lucasfilm Ltd.

ISBN 978 1 4052 7786 0
60550/1
Printed in Italy

Cover design by Richie Hull & Maddox Philpot
Designed by Jason Wojtowicz

To find more great *Star Wars* books, visit www.egmont.co.uk/starwars

A long time ago in a galaxy far, far away. . . .

The REBEL ALLIANCE has destroyed the Empire's
dreaded DEATH STAR, but the galaxy remains
convulsed by civil war, and the Imperial starfleet is
hunting the rebels throughout the galaxy.

LUKE SKYWALKER, the pilot who destroyed the
Death Star, is now hailed as a hero. But Luke seeks
only to support the freedom fighters, serving the
Rebellion behind the controls of his X-wing fighter.

Even as he flies alongside the pilots of Red Squadron,
Luke feels stirrings in the mystical energy field
known as the Force. And this farm boy turned
fighter pilot begins to suspect that his destiny
lies along a different path. . . .

PROLOGUE

JESSIKA PAVA couldn't stop staring at her X-wing fighter.

She pushed her black hair out of her eyes and sighed, forcing herself to turn around so she could no longer see the compact, deadly starfighter where it sat on its landing gear in the center of the hangar. Her fellow pilots knew she wanted nothing more than to get back into space as Blue Three.

But Jessika was on droid duty that week. Her job was to inventory the base's astromechs and make sure they were ready for duty—programming updated, flight instruments tested and confirmed as operational. It wasn't the worst job in the squadron—assisting the maintenance techs with a fuel-system cleanout was much dirtier—but Jessika was sure it was the most boring.

Her datapad beeped for her attention, and she looked down at it with a sigh, then at the cone-headed R4 unit rolling by on its three stubby legs. The droid was painted in a green-and-white checkerboard pattern, probably the work of a bored tech with time to kill.

"You there, droid," the young pilot called out. "Need you to hold up a sec for operations check."

The astromech whistled mournfully, no happier than Jessika about the need for an inspection. But it came to a stop and popped open a panel on its dome to expose a diagnostics port. Jessika aimed her datapad at the port and the pad blinked, beginning to exchange data with the droid's systems. She sat down cross-legged on the hangar deck and resigned herself to wait.

"Excuse me, but might I be of assistance?" a voice asked brightly.

Jessika looked up into the expressionless face of a protocol droid with a gold finish. It was an older model—practically an antique—with one arm clad in red plating and dozens of dings and dents.

"I don't think so, but thanks," Jessika said. "It's droid duty—the diagnostics program pretty much runs itself."

"But not terribly efficiently," said the droid, sounding disappointed. "But where are my manners? I am

See-Threepio, human-cyborg relations, at your service, Miss . . . ?"

"Pava. Jessika Pava. Blue Three."

"It is an honor to meet you, Miss Pava," Threepio said.

"Call me Blue Three."

"Oh. As you wish, Miss—I mean, Blue Three. As I said, perhaps I could be of assistance. I just installed a very exciting new Tranlang database and am fluent in nearly seven million forms of communication—including, of course, the relatively primitive languages spoken by astromechs and diagnostics readers."

The R4 unit squawked indignantly at Threepio.

"Insult you?" Threepio said, drawing back in surprise. "I did nothing of the sort, you hypersensitive little dustbin. Your method of communication *is* primitive—I was merely stating a fact. Why, you don't even have a proper vocabulator."

The R4 unit honked and swiveled its dome to stare at the protocol droid with its single electronic eye.

"Don't move," Jessika said. "You'll break the data link and then—"

Her datapad beeped plaintively.

"Now we have to start all over," she said.

The astromech hooted accusingly at Threepio.

"My fault?" Threepio replied. "Don't be ridiculous.

She told you not to move. Blue Three, might I suggest—"

"You know what, See-Threepio? I've got this. It's a simple procedure, really. I'm sure you have many more important things to do."

"You would think so, given that my specialties include communications and protocol," Threepio said. "But it so happens I have completed all my tasks for the day. I was going to suggest that this R4 unit might benefit from a memory wipe. When they start taking offense at every helpful suggestion, it's often a sign of flux in the motivator cortex."

The R4 unit blew an electronic raspberry at Threepio, but this time remained still while the diagnostic program ran. Jessika rolled her eyes as the golden droid continued to chatter away.

"Why, I often told Master Luke that Artoo's behavior would have been improved by a memory wipe. His eccentricities have been more than I can bear for decades now. One time we were on a diplomatic mission to Circarpous when—"

"Did you say Master Luke?" Jessika interrupted.

"Indeed I did," Threepio said. "Master Luke Skywalker. Do you know him?"

"Do I know Luke Skywalker?" Jessika asked incredulously, scrambling to her feet. "Of course I know him! Well, I mean, I've never met him, but *everybody* knows

Luke Skywalker. He defeated the Emperor, and they say he's the best star pilot in the galaxy."

"You'd have to ask Artoo about that. Though I must warn you that Artoo has, shall we say, an inflated view of his own accomplishments. I myself find space travel most unpleasant—"

"Wait, do you mean *Artoo-Detoo*?" Jessika asked in amazement. "The astromech that assisted Skywalker when he destroyed the first Death Star?"

Threepio cocked his golden head slightly.

"Well, yes," he said. "Artoo and I have been eyewitnesses to many momentous events during the Galactic Civil War, though he was usually off squabbling with a computer while I was performing some vital diplomatic service. With regards to the Death Star, Artoo was inoperative at the critical moment. So not even he can try to take credit for the outcome of that mission."

The datapad beeped, indicating the diagnostics program had finished running. Jessika ignored it.

"Tell me about the Death Star mission," she said. "How did Skywalker wind up destroying it?"

"It would be my pleasure, Blue Three," Threepio said. "Though that adventure began in rather dreadful fashion for me. We had crash-landed on Tatooine, with Artoo pursuing a secret mission for the Alliance in his typical stubborn manner. If not for my advice, he might still be wandering that dreadful Dune Sea—"

"On second thought, why don't you tell me that one later?" Jessika asked hastily, sensing this version was shaping up to be mostly about Threepio. "Tell me a different story about your master—one that hasn't been told a million times already."

The R4 unit chirped inquiringly at her, and she patted its dome absentmindedly.

"Your programs are up to date—report to the droid pool," she said, turning back to Threepio.

"There are so many stories," Threepio mused. "Where to begin? I know—Artoo and I were present when Master Luke first used a lightsaber in battle, not long after the Battle of Yavin."

"Tell me about that one," Jessika said.

"Very well," Threepio said. "It all began above the planet Giju, with a mission for Red Squadron. . . ."

PART
ONE

CHAPTER 01
RED SQUADRON TO THE RESCUE

LUKE SKYWALKER sensed the TIE fighter twisting for a shot at his unprotected stern even before Artoo-Detoo squealed a warning and his sensors began flashing red.

Luke didn't know *how* he knew, just that he did. His hands went automatically to the control yokes of his X-wing fighter and hauled them back and to the left, sending the craft spinning to port. Laser fire stitched space where his fighter had been a moment before, leaving Luke blinking from the brilliant glare.

"I saw him! I saw him!" Luke told Artoo even as the X-wing completed its roll and locked on to the Imperial fighter's tail. Luke mashed down the triggers and the TIE erupted into a ball of fire. Luke's X-wing shot through the cloud of dust and gas, shuddering slightly.

From the droid socket behind Luke's cockpit, Artoo let out a squeal of annoyance.

"It was *not* too close," Luke said. "You keep the fighter flying and let me worry about what to do with it."

Luke opened up the throttle and dodged a pair of freight tenders, their ion engines glowing a brilliant blue. Like many other starships above the planet Giju, they were racing away from the space lanes as fast as their engines could take them, desperate to escape the firefight that had suddenly erupted between three rebel X-wings and a patrol of TIE fighters.

Luke's eyes jumped to his long-range scopes, noting the position of the two green arrowheads on the screen. Those two symbols represented the X-wings piloted by Red Three and Red Leader. Red Leader's X-wing was in the lead, protecting a transport carrying underground rebel leaders being evacuated from Giju ahead of the Empire's agents. Reds Three and Five— Wedge Antilles and Luke—were in the rear, keeping the TIEs busy.

Wedge had drifted too far to port for Luke's liking; if his fellow pilot ran into trouble, Luke wasn't sure he could get there in time to help. And there was no shortage of trouble up there—the Empire had apparently sent every fighter it had in the system to engage the rebel raiders.

"Tighten it up, Wedge—we're each other's protection out here," Luke warned.

"Gotcha, Luke," said Wedge Antilles. "I was chasing a bandit."

"And did you get him?"

"His wingman did—flew right into him when I came up on their flank."

"That counts," Luke said.

"Less chatter, gentlemen," said the cool, clipped voice of Red Leader, known outside the cockpit as Commander Narra. "With all this traffic out here there are a lot of places for enemies to hide. You need your eyes as well as your instruments."

"Copy, Red Leader," said a chastened Luke.

Narra was a veteran pilot, tapped by Alliance High Command to lead Red Squadron after the destruction of the Death Star. Twelve Red Squadron pilots from the rebel base on Yavin 4 had headed into space in X-wings to try to destroy the Empire's battle station. Of the twelve, only Luke and Wedge had returned alive. Narra had asked them to continue to fly with Red Squadron, while making it clear that neither young man should expect special treatment for surviving an encounter with the Death Star, even if they *did* destroy it.

Which was fine with Luke; his sudden fame made him uncomfortable. Just a few months before, he'd been a farm boy on Tatooine, fixing vaporators and tinkering with skyhoppers and landspeeders. Now people treated him like some kind of hero—but he knew better. He was just a kid who'd made a million-to-one shot, guided by a mysterious power he barely understood.

Luke knew he had skill with the Force, the energy field created by life that bound the galaxy together. And now he knew he'd inherited that ability from his father. Luke's Uncle Owen had always told him that his father had been a navigator on a spice freighter, but that had been a story meant to protect Luke. Ben Kenobi had told him the real story: that Luke's father had been a Jedi Knight, a gifted star pilot and a cunning warrior. But Ben had also told Luke that his father was dead, betrayed and murdered by the Sith Lord Darth Vader. And Vader had struck down Ben aboard the Death Star just days after he'd started to teach Luke about the Force.

So Luke had skill with the Force, yes. But what good would that do him with no one left to instruct him?

"You in there, Luke?" asked Wedge, echoed by an inquiring beep from Artoo. "The boss wants us to turn to point two-two."

"Right, right," Luke said, mentally kicking himself. None of his musings about the Force would do him any good if he got himself killed—and daydreaming during a firefight was an excellent way to do that.

Luke banked to starboard until his fighter was on the course Narra wanted. Ahead of them, a line of bulk freighters was cutting across the space lanes, their bows turning every which direction as their pilots tried to avoid a collision. The ungainly ships reminded Luke of a herd of banthas huddled together for protection against predators back home on Tatooine.

"Get behind me, Wedge," Luke said. "We'll scoot and shoot."

"Right with you," Wedge said, hitting his retro-rockets and dropping astern of Luke's X-wing, then accelerating until he was flying practically on his tail. Any inbound enemies would be able to target only Luke's fighter, with Wedge scooting up and down to emerge from cover and fire at their attackers. It was a tricky maneuver—both pilots had to know each other's tendencies in combat, but more than that they had to trust each other completely. Even a month before Luke wouldn't have dared to try it, but since then he'd flown numerous missions with Wedge. They could now fly in perfect formation, anticipating each other's movements without speaking a word.

"Artoo, switch the deflectors to double front," Luke said, ignoring the astromech's sulky beep that he'd already done so.

He rolled across the topside of one of the bulk freighters, then dove beneath the next one, juking and weaving to throw off any Imperial that might be trying to get a bead on him. Ahead, three TIEs wheeled through space, green fire lancing out from their blaster cannons. Laser fire splashed against Luke's shields, which flared with the impact. Luke broke to starboard while Wedge broke to port, their cannons spitting energy. One of the TIEs vanished in a fountain of fire, while another lurched drunkenly, one solar panel bent and spraying sparks. The third TIE was rising, up and away from the fight.

"Wedge! Down!"

Luke thrust his stick forward, throwing the X-wing into a dive that slammed him back in his seat, grunting with effort. Laser blasts burst all around him, dazzling his eyes. He dodged left, then right, ignoring Artoo's flurry of protests. He had no time to peer at his readout and see if Wedge was still alive, or if his X-wing had been turned into a superheated cloud by the quartet of TIEs that had been lurking in the heart of the freighter convoy, waiting to ambush them.

"How did you—" Wedge began, then stopped. "You know, for just an hour I'd like to know what it's like to fly with the Force watching my back."

"It's almost as good as having you watching my back," Luke said with a grin. "Now let's make them pay for that little trick. Artoo, dial up the inertial compensators."

Luke slewed his fighter around in a tight turn, grimacing at the sound of some overstressed system groaning in the port wing. Wedge followed him, weaving around Luke's X-wing and filling the space ahead of them with deadly spears of light. Two laser blasts ripped one of the TIEs in half, while another flew too close to a freighter's engine wash and tumbled out of control.

"Two left," Luke said. "I'll take the one to port."

He opened up the throttle, and the distance between him and the TIE ahead began to shrink. To starboard, he could see Wedge's fighter matching his maneuver. The TIE dodged in every direction, the pilot's desperation increasingly obvious, but Luke hung right on his tail.

And then . . . what was that? It felt like something was in his mind, something elusive. Like a word he couldn't quite call to mind even though it was on the tip of his tongue. Artoo whistled urgently and Luke shook his head, trying to chase the odd feeling away. There were more pressing matters at hand.

Wedge rolled down and right, then up and left, bracketing the TIE in his sights. A moment later the Imperial fighter he'd been chasing was a bright cloud in their wake as they continued to race up and away from Giju.

"You need a little help there, Red Five?" Wedge asked.

Luke smacked the side of his helmet, annoyed with himself. He needed to focus.

"I've got it, thanks," he said, rolling his fighter completely over and blasting the TIE's starboard panel off with a volley of shots while flying upside down. He brought the X-wing right side up as the crippled TIE tumbled past him, the cockpit oscillating wildly around its remaining solar panel. Then Luke settled his X-wing in beside Wedge's, their wingtips just meters apart.

"I was just asking," Wedge said. "No need to get fancy."

Artoo squawked derisively.

"Nice flying," Narra said in their ears. "The package is clear and calculating the jump into hyperspace. Activate your scatter protocols and we'll meet at the rendezvous point at 2300 hours."

"Copy that, boss," Wedge said. "Activating protocol now. See you on the other side, Luke."

A moment later Narra's X-wing vanished into the infinity of hyperspace, followed by Wedge's.

"Access the jump pattern for Devaron, Artoo," Luke said.

Rebel procedure was for each pilot to follow a randomly chosen zigzag path through hyperspace, making several jumps to foil any Imperials that might be tracking his or her fighter. That way, if the worst occurred, only one fighter would be lost instead of a whole squadron—or the entire rebel fleet.

Artoo beeped at Luke that he'd accessed the coordinates and locked them into the navicomputer, then followed that up with a fusillade of hoots and whistles. Luke glanced at his screen, where the little droid's communications were translated into language he could understand.

"I'm sure there will be patrols searching for us—the Empire's flooding sectors with warships in response to any threat," Luke said. "That's why we follow scatter protocol."

Luke missed whatever Artoo whistled in response—that feeling was back in his head again, like a voice whose words he couldn't quite make out. He knew it was the Force. But this time, it wasn't assisting his actions. Instead, it felt like it was trying to get his attention.

"What's that, Artoo? Yes, I'm functioning normally. But you can take over flight duties till we get to Devaron."

Artoo beeped questioningly.

"I'm fine, pal," Luke said. "Honest. But take the stick anyway. I want to try meditating while we're in hyperspace. Maybe that will help me figure out what it is the Force keeps trying to tell me."

CHAPTER 02
THE CALL OF THE FORCE

OUTSIDE LUKE'S COCKPIT, hyperspace was an ever-changing tunnel of brilliant light. Inside, the rebel pilot had his eyes closed and was breathing slowly in and out.

During their brief time as master and student, Ben Kenobi had taught him the basics of Jedi meditation, warning him that opening a connection to the Force was something even the eldest Jedi Masters studied over a lifetime. Luke's first lesson had come just hours after the murder of his aunt and uncle by stormtroopers, when Luke and Ben had stopped for the night on their way to Mos Eisley.

Ben had told him to focus on whatever emotions were uppermost in his mind, being honest with himself about the feelings he was experiencing and how they were affecting him. And then, one by one, he was to let each emotion go, like pouring out a cup of water. The goal was to make himself an empty vessel. Only then, Ben had said, would the Force be able to fill him.

What emotions was he feeling? Luke considered the question. He was excited about the successful completion of their mission—that was in his mind. And he was anxious—the Force was trying to tell him something, but he had no teacher to help him interpret its messages.

What had happened to Ben Kenobi? The old Jedi's body had vanished the moment Darth Vader's lightsaber blade touched him, leaving nothing but dusty robes on the floor. Luke had cried out in grief and rage, firing at the stormtroopers and Vader. But then he'd heard Ben's voice in his head, telling him to run. He'd heard that voice again above the Death Star, urging him to let the Force tell him when to take his shot at the battle station's vulnerable thermal exhaust port, instead of using his targeting computer.

But he hadn't heard Ben's voice since—and he feared he never would again.

Luke pushed the thought gently away. *Don't center on your anxieties—keep your concentration here and now, where it belongs.* Ben had taught him that, too.

He examined each emotion in turn—first the excitement, then the anxiety—and then he imagined himself pouring them out, to vanish amid the whirling tumult of hyperspace. For a long time, he simply sat in the cockpit and let his mind drift.

There was green grass under his feet. No, not grass—stones. He was standing on flagstones, but they were so overgrown with grass that at first he'd thought he was standing in some kind of meadow. Trees had grown up through the stones, forming a glade in what had once been a courtyard.

He heard water nearby. He turned and saw a fountain, surrounded by statues of people in robes. They were faceless and without limbs— they'd been sheared off by energy weapons, the surfaces blackened. The fountain was destroyed, too—but water still burbled up from inside it, spilling out through the broken walls and across the glade.

Something made a strange noise, a little like the lowing of a bantha or a dewback. Among the trees, birds and insects flitted between branches. Beyond them stood a group of horned animals, their sides gray and scaly.

He realized his lightsaber was in his hand. And then he sensed something else. He looked up and saw three remotes hovering nearby— remotes like the one Han Solo had kept for blaster target practice aboard the Millennium Falcon.

Three? He couldn't fend off three—he had enough trouble anticipating the actions of just one. But the Force was very strong there. He could feel it all around him, a living thing, like wind or rain.

And it was telling him that something wasn't right.

The horned creatures were pawing at the grass, muttering in distress.

And then he could feel it. Something dark and wicked was nearby, bent on his destruction.

He slipped on a loose flagstone, nearly falling to his knees before he recovered his balance—

—and found himself gazing into the infinite kaleidoscope of hyperspace. He was breathing heavily, he realized, and sweat was running into his eyes behind his goggles.

Artoo tootled something, and Luke glanced at the translation on his screen.

"I know my heart rate is up—I can feel that myself," he said. "But I'm okay now. It was the Force. It was showing me something—a vision, I guess you'd say."

But what did the vision mean? He'd been practicing with his lightsaber, in a place where the Force surrounded him. Yet his life had been in danger. If only the vision had lasted a moment longer, perhaps he might have learned what it meant instead of having to guess.

His screen lit up with a series of messages from Artoo.

Luke laughed.

"I agree the Force would be more useful if it gave me an actual message instead of random data," he said. "But that's not how it works. I'll just have to keep my mind open and hope the next thing it tells me is easier to understand."

————

A refueling station hung above the mottled green-and-yellow sphere of Devaron, its navigational lights blinking green and red against the stars. Luke took back the controls from Artoo and guided his X-wing down toward the station and the pitted bulk of an ancient freighter nestled against it.

Artoo tweetled happily and Luke nodded: his sensors showed two X-wings attached to the freighter's underside.

"Looks like Narra and Wedge beat us here," he said.

"Approaching starfighter, identify," said a stern voice over the comm.

"Little Brother Five coming home to Mama," Luke said.

"Acknowledged," the voice said, its tone more friendly now. "Nice to have the family back together."

Luke eased the X-wing beneath the freighter, goosing the retrorockets as a flexible docking tube descended from the larger ship's underside, like the questing tentacle of some great beast. The tube locked itself over the X-wing's cockpit and droid socket, clamping tight. Once Artoo tweeted that they were successfully docked, Luke popped his cockpit's canopy and clambered up a flexible ladder in the tube, waving to Artoo where he waited in the fighter's droid socket.

He emerged in the freighter's main hold, where

Narra and Wedge were waiting for him, their flight helmets under their arms.

"Sorry I'm late," Luke said, relieved to finally shed his own helmet. He'd spent much of his childhood dreaming about flying a fighter in deep space, yet somehow none of those fantasies had included the fact that helmets smelled awful, left you sweaty, and gave you a headache.

"You're not late," Narra said. "The Alliance has assigned you a more complicated scatter pattern, with additional jumps."

"Flyboys like us are a credit a dozen," Wedge said. "Heroes like you get special treatment."

Wedge grinned to show he was kidding, but Luke's face fell anyway. His life shouldn't be more important than the lives of his fellow Red Squadron pilots.

Narra clapped Luke on the shoulder and smiled.

"You won't like *this* special treatment, son," he said. "Orders direct from the fleet—Mon Mothma's asked you to retrieve logs of Imperial communications that were intercepted by several rebel cells along the Shipwrights' Trace."

Luke groaned. All he wanted to do was fly his X-wing against the Empire, not fetch data tapes. But he couldn't ignore an order from the Alliance's leader.

"Those logs could give us a picture of Imperial operations on the entire trade route," Narra said. "Think of it as your chance to see the galaxy, Lieutenant Skywalker. The mission details have been loaded into your astromech. He's on his way to Docking Bay 12 to do preflight on your Y-wing—you'll be flying Y 4, one of the two-seat models."

Luke scowled. The Y-wings were ungainly fighters, slower and less maneuverable than X-wings. And the two-seat configuration suggested someone from the Alliance was coming with him—he hoped it wasn't some member of the diplomatic corps who'd spend the journey practicing speeches and getting spacesick.

The doors to the hold opened, and a droid with gold plating walked stiffly into the hangar beside a dull gray supervisor droid with red photoreceptors.

"I don't know why this is so difficult for you to process," See-Threepio said angrily. "As a translator, my skills are essential to the success of this mission. That means a weekly oil bath is well within allowable regulations, and the quality of the lubricant used is critically important."

The supervisor droid grumbled something as it trudged along.

"Then you need to have your calibration rechecked," Threepio said. "The oil you have onboard might date back to the First Coruscani Migration. If it got any sludgier it would actually be solid."

"Good luck, Skywalker," Narra said with a

smile. Luke wasn't sure whether he was referring to the recruiting mission or the chances of surviving Threepio's complaints.

"Yeah, Luke—enjoy your flying brick," Wedge said.

The two Reds turned away, but then Narra stopped and looked over his shoulder, his expression grave.

"Watch out for Imperial patrols, Skywalker," he said. "Devaron's lightly garrisoned, but it's not too far from Giju. We just embarrassed the Empire—I wouldn't be surprised if they threw a dragnet over this entire region."

Luke nodded, then turned to where Threepio was waiting with ill-concealed impatience.

"Nice to see you again, Threepio," he said to the gleaming droid. "What were you saying?"

"I was explaining that I've prepared a dossier for each of our three stops on this mission, Master Luke," Threepio said. "I'm particularly excited to visit Whiforla II. Whiforla-song is one of the six million forms of communication in which I am fluent, and among the most complex. I can instruct you in the proper fluting for ceremonial introductions to the rebel leaders there, though as a human your vocal range will limit you to basic greetings and congratulations on a successful molting. I'm afraid this will force us to cut the exchange of well wishes to less than an hour."

"That *is* a shame," Luke said.

"Oh, I quite agree, Master Luke," Threepio said brightly. "I thought on the way to our docking bay we could start practicing the first of the four Whiforlan fluting forms."

The corridors of the refueling station were filled with a mix of species—horned Devaronians rubbed shoulders with green-skinned Duros, while diminutive Aleena dodged massive Herglics. The blank walls were interrupted here and there by windows revealing Devaron below.

Luke had shed his flight suit and put on a yellow jacket, black shirt, and brown trousers—the kind of clothes worn by spacers across the galaxy. His blaster pistol sat snug in a holster on his hip, while his father's lightsaber hung beneath his jacket, concealed from view.

Luke stiffened as he spotted a quartet of stormtroopers marching in his direction, led by an officer in an olive-green uniform. The spacers in the corridor gave the troopers a wide berth, shrinking from them with fearful looks.

"Oh my, stormtroopers," Threepio said. "As dangerous fugitives we'll surely be captured and sent to some terrible prison. I hope it's not the—"

"Shh," Luke said. "There's no reason to suspect us of anything. Remember our cover story—we're hyperspace scouts. Honest, hardworking hyperspace scouts."

But Luke had to fight down a surge of anger at the sight of the troopers' gleaming white armor. Back on Tatooine, soldiers like these had killed his aunt and uncle and turned the only home he'd ever known into a smoking ruin. And they'd done similar things to countless other families on thousands and thousands of other planets.

He kept his expression blank as he walked past the troopers, with Threepio clanking along behind him. He'd almost relaxed when he heard the clipped, cold voice of the officer.

"You there! Halt!"

Luke stopped and turned slowly, hoping the troopers were stopping someone else. But the officer was looking right at him, finger pointed accusingly.

"Hand over your identification," the man said.

Luke carefully reached into his jacket pocket—the stormtroopers might have itchy trigger fingers, and the death of a civilian on a refueling station would require nothing more than a report to be buried in a bureaucratic archive somewhere. He extracted his identification and handed it to the officer, whose eyes jumped between it and Luke's face as Threepio fidgeted nearby, his servomotors whining.

"Your purpose here?" the officer asked as he slid Luke's ID through a slot in his datapad.

Luke wished desperately that he had Ben Kenobi's ability to cloud minds with the Force. But that knowledge had vanished along with the old Jedi's body. He'd have to hope that the Alliance's slicers had created a fake identity good enough to fool the Empire.

Well, he could rely on hope and a bit of acting. He'd seen Han bluff his way past his share of Imperial patrols, after all.

"Hyperspace scout, just like it says there," Luke said, trying to pack a bit of Corellian bluster into his voice. "We're refuelin' before we head out to the Western Reaches. Friend of a friend found an ol' ship log, see—a ship log with the coordinates of a Tibanna gas deposit. Interstellar gas—the really pure stuff."

Luke told himself to stop and blink suspiciously at the officer.

"But don't go jumpin' my claim now," Luke muttered, shaking a finger in warning. "Wouldn't be proper."

"We have no interest in your lunatic tales about space gas," the officer said. "And where is your scout ship?"

"Docking Bay 42, just down the hall here," Luke said. "Bought me a converted starfighter—Clone Wars salvage, modified for long hauls. She's a tough ol' gal—rode out a meteorite strike in the Lower Flora Cloud with just a couple of dents. Lower Flora's where we got jumped by Sikurdian pirates, you know. Say, you fellas mind taggin' along? We could throw a scare into them bandits—"

"Be quiet," the officer snapped. "I am an officer of the Galactic Empire, not some scruffy mercenary for you to hire."

"It was just a suggestion," Luke said plaintively.

The officer glared at Luke, then eyed Threepio, who fidgeted uncomfortably.

"And what does a hyperspace scout need with a protocol droid?"

"Oh, this one can talk to anything—he's programmed with about a million strange Wild Space dialects and old trade languages."

"Six million, to be exact—" Threepio began.

"Plus I've made a few special modifications," Luke interrupted. "Even taught him to cook a not-bad pot of chuba stew. No need for that look, sir! Chubas ain't just Hutt chow, you know. That's an unfortunate misconception. See, what you need to do is season them—"

The officer held up his hand for silence and thrust Luke's identification back at him.

"Carry on," he said. "But remember, it's the duty of every Imperial citizen to report suspicious activity. In any region."

Luke nodded and the officer signaled to the storm-troopers, who marched away.

"Thank goodness," Threepio said. "I'm not pro-grammed to resist interrogation."

"I wasn't looking forward to it either," Luke said as he and Threepio continued toward the docking bay where Artoo was waiting.

Then Luke stopped at one of the windows over-looking Devaron, Threepio nearly plowing into him.

"Master Luke, what is it?"

Luke didn't answer, continuing to stare at Devaron. Someone or something down there was calling to him.

"Sir? Are you quite all right?"

Luke shushed the droid and reached out with his mind in hopes of figuring out what the Force was ask-ing him to do. Was Devaron where he was supposed to go? Was it somehow connected with his vision?

But he could sense nothing else. He turned away from the green-and-yellow planet with a frown.

"We need to get to our fighter if we're to make the first rendezvous," Luke said. "And we wouldn't want to keep Artoo waiting, now would we?"

CHAPTER 03
THE HAND OF THE EMPIRE

AS HIS Y-WING FIGHTER climbed away from the refueling station, Luke glanced back down at Devaron, hoping for some new signal from the Force. He was still staring at the jungles far below when Artoo beeped to get his attention.

"Sorry, Artoo," Luke said. "Access the jump pattern for Whiforla."

"Space travel used to be so much more civilized," Threepio groused from where he sat in the tail gunner's bubble behind Luke. "One could simply travel from place to place, rather than meandering about like a Purcassian river eel during spawning season."

"Well, a more civilized galaxy is what we're fighting for," Luke said as the Y-wing rocketed into hyperspace.

"I hadn't thought of it that way," Threepio said.

"I for one will be much more comfortable when the Rebellion wins, then."

On this flight the churning infinity of faster-than-light travel brought Luke no comfort—his anxieties seemed to press in on him despite his attempts to empty his mind of them. What had the Force been trying to tell him back there above Devaron? Should he have waited for the strange feeling to return?

Perhaps the Force was trying to tell him that he was supposed to be learning to command its power instead of fetching communications logs. Learning the ways of the Force was what his father had done with his life—and the legacy Ben Kenobi had preserved for two decades on Tatooine, passing it along with the lightsaber that Luke's father had wanted him to have. And there he was worrying about proper Whiforlan fluting.

What if the Force was trying to stop him from making a mistake?

The rebel scatter program brought Luke's Y-wing out of hyperspace in the Tertiary Usaita system, which was little more than a sparse collection of dust and rock around a red dwarf, marked by a navigational beacon left there thousands of years before by a long-dead Republic survey team.

It was a lonely place—but not, as it turned out, an empty one.

"Unknown fighter, this is the *Kreuge's Revenge*," a voice said in Luke's cockpit. "This is a restricted system. Shut down all flight systems and prepare for inspection."

"Artoo, calculate the next jump and get us out of here!" Luke said.

Artoo whistled an acknowledgment, and Luke threw the control yoke hard right, grimacing at how sluggishly the Y-wing responded. His sensor scope lit up, and his eyes took in the information: three TIE fighters, backed up by a *Razor*-class frigate.

"Oh no!" squealed Threepio. "We're in danger! Artoo, do something!"

"Hang on, Threepio," Luke said sternly.

He turned to the navigational heading Artoo gave him and opened up the Y-wing's throttle, trying to coax every bit of speed out of the heavy fighter. But moments later brilliant flashes of light erupted around them and the Y-wing shuddered.

The three TIEs raced overhead, and Luke squeezed the trigger, peppering them with laser fire as they wheeled around for another pass.

"How long, Artoo?" he asked.

Artoo whistled and hooted.

"A *minute*?" Threepio shrieked. "What do you mean you're triangulating our position? This isn't the time for stargazing, you miserable lump of circuits!"

Luke rolled the Y-wing to port, eyes jumping from

his long-range scanners to the TIEs angling in on him. He tried to summon the Force, to let it guide his hands. But Threepio's chatter and the flashes of laser fire kept throwing off his concentration. The Y-wing's starboard shields flared as the TIEs' lasers struck home, and alarms began to blare.

"Artoo, divert the power," Luke said, hammering at the Imperial fighters with the Y-wing's turret guns. The more maneuverable Imperials were wheeling in all directions now, swooping in on their slower target.

Focus, Luke told himself. *Use the Force.*

He rolled the Y-wing over to starboard, trying to protect the vulnerable shield, and mashed down on the triggers. One of the TIEs vanished in a cloud of flames. But almost immediately, another fighter streaked up from beneath him, its laser cannons raking the Y-wing's hull. The starboard shield flickered and died—and with it, Luke felt his connection to the Force slipping.

The frigate was peppering them with blasts now, too, bouncing the fighter up and down. Luke squeezed off a flurry of shots at one of the remaining fighters, forcing its pilot to abandon his attack run. But his wingman took advantage of Luke's distraction to drop behind the Y-wing. Green flashes lit up space as the TIE fighter's blasts ripped through the starboard engine. Red lights blinked frantically on Luke's control panel.

"Try to increase the power!" he yelled, firing desperately at the two fighters hunting him, and weaving left and right in an effort to throw off the Imperials' aim.

The starboard engine's power levels climbed, then plummeted. Laser fire knocked the fighter sideways. The TIE that had hit them streaked away from the Y-wing, cut right, then turned and raced back toward them, aiming at the battered fighter's defenseless starboard side.

"This is the end," Threepio moaned.

Luke fired at the TIE, but the Imperial pilot refused to deviate from his course. He kept coming, waiting to line up the shot that would destroy the engine and leave the Y-wing helpless in space. Luke tried to turn away, but the fighter was barely responding.

I'm sorry, Ben, he thought. *I'm sorry, Father. I tried my best.*

He braced for impact—

—and was shoved back into his chair as the Y-wing shot into the safety of hyperspace.

Artoo beeped, perhaps a bit smugly.

"Well, you certainly took your time about it," Threepio grumbled.

As the two droids continued their long-running

argument, Luke exhaled in mingled gratitude and disbelief. But there was no time to waste. The Y-wing was barely flying—they'd been saved by the tough old fighter's ability to soak up damage, but they needed to find a spaceport in which to make repairs. And they needed to do it quickly.

Luke rejected Artoo's first choice for a starport, then the next three. All were either too far away or tightly controlled by the Empire.

"That's enough, Artoo," he said. "We're going back to Devaron."

Artoo whistled an objection.

"But, Master Luke, our mission—" Threepio began.

"Send an encrypted message to the fleet," he said. "Tell them I'll resume the retrieval mission after we repair our fighter."

Artoo started to hoot at him, but Luke shook his head.

"No, my mind's made up—take us to Devaron."

That's where the Force was telling me to go, Luke thought. *This time I'm going to listen.*

CHAPTER 04
RETURN TO DEVARON

THE Y-WING FLEW LOW over the thick jungles of Devaron, a ribbon of smoke trailing from its damaged engine. Luke had shushed the droids and sought to clear his mind of doubts and questions, letting the Force direct the fighter's flight. It had guided him into the atmosphere on the far side of the planet from the capital and its Imperial garrison, then across the outback. Below him, the jungle was broken by outcroppings of stone that rose high above the surrounding trees, crowned with enormous vines and creepers. The light of the late-afternoon sun turned the rivers into threads of brilliant orange and pink.

Luke turned the Y-wing to starboard. Ahead was another pair of rocky pillars. . . . No, that wasn't correct, Luke saw now. This was something different. The rocky pillars were artificial structures—towers made by intelligent hands.

Luke eased up on the throttle, and something began banging inside the battered engine. The tops of the towers were jagged, stabbing into the sky, and their sides were pocked with craters.

That's blast damage, Luke thought. *From heavy weapons. They really took a beating.*

"Artoo, look for a place to set down near those towers," Luke said. "This is where we're supposed to go. I know it is."

Artoo hooted urgently. Luke glanced at the screen and frowned.

"I understand you can barely keep the fighter in the air," he said. "But this is important."

"Master Luke, are you sure that's the wisest choice?" Threepio asked. "Artoo says he can land our ship, but doubts he can get it airborne again. We must find a place for repairs."

Luke sighed. Threepio had a point. Surely the Force wasn't telling him to maroon himself in the middle of the jungle.

"You're right—it will have to wait," he said. "Scan the area for signs of settlement—and listen for activity on Imperial communications channels."

———

The town was little more than a cluster of buildings atop a plateau in the jungle, with a landing field whose single beacon winked in the gloom of dusk. A massive spire of bare gray stone rose a hundred meters into the air on one side of the town, crowning a steep, forested slope. On the other side of the plateau the trees had been cleared and the hill carved into terraced farmers' fields.

Luke flew low over the town—his fighter's data file said it was called Tikaroo—and peered down at the landing field.

"I mostly see atmosphere fliers down there," he said. "No sign of any Imperial ships. But there are a couple of star yachts parked off to the side. That one looks like a SoroSuub 3000. That's a pretty fancy ship to find near a farm town in the middle of nowhere."

"Perhaps the last harvest was particularly rewarding," said Threepio.

Luke shook his head.

"Farmers don't spend their credits on star yachts," he said. "They save their money so they don't starve when they have a bad year."

Artoo hooted.

"Oh, switch off," Threepio said. "Like you know anything about agriculture, you oversize screwdriver."

Luke decided that solving this particular mystery

would have to wait—his choice was to set down in Tikaroo or crash in the jungle. He activated the retrorockets and set the Y-wing down with a jolt, followed by a hiss of coolant venting from some punctured reservoir.

The air was wet and ripe with vegetation. Light spilled from the open doorway of a squat building at the end of the landing field. Luke descended from the cockpit and patted the Y-wing's hull gratefully, then strolled across the landing field as the droids extricated themselves from the fighter.

A Devaronian male met him at the door, wiping his hands on a rag. Behind him, a teenage Devaronian girl looked up from a cluttered workbench, scowling beneath her polarized goggles.

"Name's Korl Marcus," Luke said after a tense moment in which he couldn't remember what it said on his false identification. "I'm a hyperspace scout. My droids and I ran into a little pirate trouble a couple of systems over, and we need some repairs."

"I'm Kivas," the Devaronian said. "That's my daughter, Farnay. Let me get a light and we'll take a look at your problem."

Kivas fetched a work light, and Luke followed him across the landing field, where the droids were waiting.

"Hello, sir," Threepio said. "I am See-Threepio, human-cyborg relations. And this is—"

"No need to be so formal, Threepio," Luke said hastily. "Let the man work."

Kivas let the light play over the Y-wing's twisted hull and peered into the craters blasted into its plating. The holes in the starboard engine were fringed with beads where laser blasts had liquefied the metal.

"Pirate trouble, eh?" he said with a smirk. "Should probably report that to the Imperial governor."

"I probably should," Luke said, giving Threepio a warning glance. "Did I mention I have credits?"

"Always good to hear," Kivas said. "I can repair this with what I have in the shop. But it will take three or four days—and six thousand credits. All in advance."

"Six thousand?" Threepio gasped. "Master L—um, Korl, this man does not run a reputable business. I suggest we—"

"That will do, Threepio," Luke said. "Six thousand? Really?"

"It would cost less if I had replacement parts shipped in from the capital," Kivas said with a shrug. "But then there'd be a lot of paperwork. Permits, bureaucrats asking questions, that sort of thing."

"Oh, there's enough paperwork in the galaxy as it is," Luke said smoothly, reaching for his credit chip. "Let's not trouble the authorities—surely the Empire has more important things to worry about than repairs to a scout ship."

"I'll get your fighter under cover, then," Kivas said, showing a mouthful of pointed teeth. "Town's that way—you can take a room at the depot with the others."

The depot was a rambling building in the center of Tikaroo, assembled seemingly at random from wood, stone, prefab plastic buildings, and shipping containers emblazoned with the faded logos of Corellian import-export firms. A long porch looked out over shuttered shops and food stalls. Landspeeders, speeder bikes, and a trio of squat, green-skinned pack beasts awaited their owners out front.

Luke followed the buzz of conversation and music through a pair of swinging doors and into a wide common room crowded with tables, mismatched chairs, and couches, many of which had seen better decades. Faces turned his way as he entered, with Threepio following uncertainly behind. There were men and women from a dozen different species, though at least half of those gathered were Devaronians. A few wore rich clothes, but most were clad in worn, practical garments.

"Hey, Porst! Fresh meat!" one of the Devaronians yelled as Luke made his way across the room to a counter crowded with bottles of brightly colored liquid. Some of the liquids were fizzing or roiling in a way he found alarming. "Man needs a room! And probably a guide!"

A Rodian missing one of his antennae began pounding on a buzzer set into the top of the counter, grinning at Luke. After a moment an old Devaronian with an eye patch emerged from a curtained alcove, looking Luke up and down. He named an exorbitant price for a room.

"That's fine," Luke said before Threepio could risk another short circuit. Both Porst and the onlookers seemed slightly disappointed—apparently they'd been looking forward to a lively bout of haggling.

"Next customer was mine—we rolled a chance-cube for it, remember?" the Rodian warned the young Devaronian standing next to him at the counter. Then he turned to Luke.

"Name's Opato, good sir—and I'm the best guide in Tikaroo," he said. "Bagged pikhrons on my last three hunts. Satisfaction guaranteed or you get a third of your credits back."

"What's a—" Luke began.

"My green friend here couldn't guide you out of a sack if you cut the bottom out of it first," the young Devaronian interrupted.

"Sir, be wary!" Opato exclaimed. "This one's the biggest liar in Tikaroo—and that's saying something!"

The Devaronian smiled at Luke.

"You need a native—someone like Duna Hilaris. That's me. I've been exploring this jungle since I was a boy. I'm famous for knowing every pool, sand pit, and shady glade the pikhrons like to visit."

"Glad to hear it," Luke said. "But what's a pikhron?"

When the laughter showed no signs of stopping, Threepio sidled up to Luke.

"My data file on this planet is basic, but apparently pikhrons are native herbivores. Their skins and teeth fetch considerable prices on the black market, as hunting them is forbidden by Imperial decree."

"Lots of things are forbidden around here but happen anyway," Duna said. "Don't make your master worry, tin man. We've got an arrangement with the governor."

"I'm not much of a hunter, but I could use a guide," Luke said. "I want to visit the towers I saw on my way in. The ruined ones?"

The crowd fell silent, even the clank of utensils on dinner plates stopping. The music burbled merrily along uninterrupted. A puzzled Luke looked from face to face.

"Eedit's off limits," Porst said.

Luke smiled. "I thought many things were forbidden in Tikaroo but happened anyway."

The joke fell flat—Opato took a sudden interest in

his drink, Duna checked his comlink, and the other guides turned away.

"Was it something I said?" Luke asked.

"No one goes to Eedit," Porst said. "You'd bring ruin to us all, messing with that place. It would risk everything we have left."

"Why? I don't understand."

"Because it's cursed, you brainless outlander," growled a massive, mean-looking slab of humanoid muscle. "Filled with the ghosts of the—"

Porst made a slashing motion across his throat, his single eye cold and staring.

"All you need to know is to stay away from it," he said, handing Luke his room key. "Number twelve upstairs. House rules are on the back of the door, but here's the most important one: I don't tolerate troublemakers. And you're already on my bad side, outlander."

"Think I'll turn in, then," Luke said. "Maybe we can make a fresh start tomorrow."

Porst just turned away.

The room was simple but clean, with a balcony overlooking Tikaroo. Luke stared up at the stars while Threepio fussed over the room's power connectors, certain he and Artoo would be incinerated the second they tried to recharge.

No moons were in the sky. Luke couldn't remember if Devaron had any.

"I for one will be grateful to be back with the Alliance," Threepio said. "I know you're disappointed not to find a guide, Master Luke, but no doubt it's for the best. I almost think I'd prefer getting shot at by the Empire to a suicidal trek into jungles prowled by savage beasts."

Luke just smiled. He wasn't afraid of jungle beasts, and he didn't believe in curses. He'd reach the towers. He just hadn't figured out how yet.

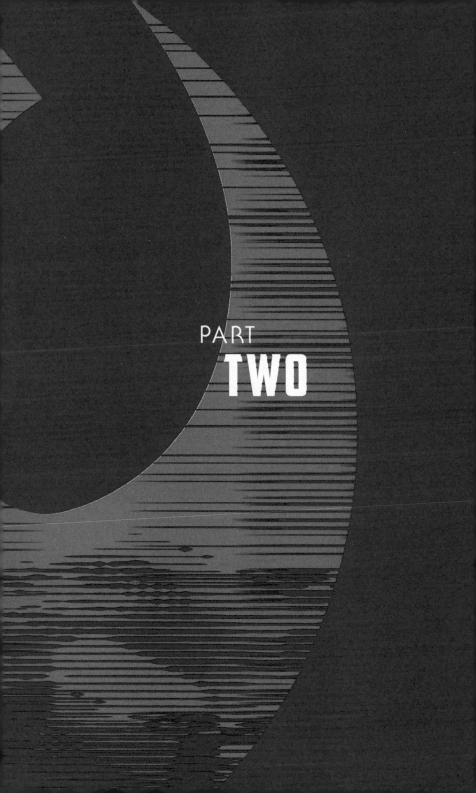

PART
TWO

CHAPTER 05
VISION OF THE PAST

H E WAS SWIMMING *in dark water, beneath two pale moons in a sky spangled with stars.*

He moved through the water with smooth, easy strokes, alternately gliding along the surface and dipping beneath it. When he got tired he surfaced and treaded water gently until the ripples he'd created ebbed, turning the water into a mirror of the night sky. He looked down at the water and saw his face looking back—except it wasn't his face. His reflection had black eyes and mottled gray-and-green skin wreathed by tentacles.

He dove, powerful kicks of his feet taking him deep beneath the water. He inhaled water but didn't choke—the oxygen in it revitalized him. He smiled. It was peaceful down there below the surface—a realm of pleasantly cool water and muted sound.

A rock wall loomed ahead of him, with a dark oval cut in the middle of it. He swam down into it, then up through a twisting corridor. His feet found purchase on stone steps, and his head broke the surface of the water. At the top of the stairs stood a human in dark gray and brown robes. He was holding a lightsaber, which he held out with a smile.

Luke awoke with a start, sitting up in the bed in his room in the Tikaroo depot. It was dark, and the night thrummed with the song of insects. Threepio sat on a bench against the wall, his photoreceptors dark as he recharged, but Luke saw the red light of Artoo's processing indicator turn his way, followed by a curious beep.

"I was swimming," he said, and Artoo whistled questioningly.

"In my dream, of course," Luke said, trying to clear the fog from his brain. "I can't swim. Not much use for it on Tatooine. But in the dream I could."

Artoo offered a baffled hoot, and Luke smiled.

"Because in the dream I was someone else," he said, scrubbing his hands through his messy hair. "I don't understand it either."

He swung his feet to the floor and walked out onto the balcony. Just a few lights shone in sleeping Tikaroo. Luke looked up into the night and saw two pale moons above.

He immediately recognized them as the same ones he'd seen in his dream, even down to their positions in the sky. The constellations were identical, too.

Devaron. I was dreaming of Devaron. No, not dreaming. It was the Force, giving me another clue about where to go.

Luke leaned on the railing of the balcony and stared

out past the great spire on the edge of town, a darker shape against the starry sky.

There was a lake out there in the jungle—a lake an alien Jedi had swum in. And that lake hid a passageway.

Now he knew where he was supposed to go.

Porridge and tarine tea made for a warm, filling breakfast, but Luke got a chilly reception from Porst, and the guides all curtly informed him that they weren't for hire.

Angry, he stomped out through the depot's swinging doors into the streets of Tikaroo, with Threepio shuffling hurriedly after him—Luke had sent Artoo to the landing field to check on how Kivas was doing with the repairs.

The villagers glanced at him curiously as he marched through the town, imagining and rejecting various ideas—flying the repaired Y-wing into the jungle, say, or trusting an uncertain combination of Artoo's sensors and his own shaky command of the Force. He knew neither of those plans was a good one, and the other ideas he came up with were even worse.

There was no help for it—he'd have to go back to the depot and tell the guides that since credits were no object, they should name their price. Surely one of them would be greedy enough to risk a journey to the forbidden towers.

Threepio tapped him on the shoulder.

"Master Luke, I believe that girl from the landing field has been following us."

Luke glanced back and spotted a slim Devaronian figure with spots on her forehead ducking around the corner of a house. He sighed and strode off in that direction.

Farnay had pressed herself against the wall. She glared at him when he arrived, taking one step to run but then thinking better of it.

"First of all, I wasn't following you," she said.

"Who said you were?" Luke asked with a smile.

Color bloomed in Farnay's cheeks, beneath her thin covering of reddish down.

"All right, maybe I was."

"That's better," Luke said. "I don't think you're cut out to be a spy—you just got caught by See-Threepio."

Farnay scowled. "I . . . I trailed you to the depot last night and heard you asking about the towers—and about Eedit. I could've warned you how they'd react."

Threepio came clanking up behind Luke, complaining about mud in his joints.

"You know about Eedit?" Luke asked. "What is it?"

"Just a bunch of ruins. But the Empire doesn't allow anyone to go there. It was a temple for the sorcerers in the old war—before they tried to take over the galaxy and had to be destroyed."

Luke winced at hearing the Emperor's lie on the lips of this young girl. But the Imperial propaganda was less important than what Farnay had revealed. The towers were a Jedi temple—and the Force was calling him there.

"So the guides won't go there because the Empire forbids it?" Luke asked.

"Well, that and it's haunted—that's the story, anyway."

"Haunted? By what?"

"By the spirits of those who died there," Farnay said. "They say in the end the sorcerers summoned a demon warrior to help them defend against the machines— only the spell went wrong. So the demon killed them and imprisoned them there forever."

"A demon?" Threepio said. "Oh dear."

Luke raised an eyebrow, and Farnay shrugged.

"I don't believe it either," she said. "I think the guides like telling that story better than admitting that they're all too afraid of Porst—he owns most of the equipment in Tikaroo, and if you cross him he won't rent to you. But I can take you there. I know the way. I don't believe in demons, and I'm not afraid of ghosts."

Luke must have looked skeptical, because Farnay stamped her foot impatiently.

"Think I can't? I've led hunting parties into the jungle plenty of times, you know. I've got my own hunting rifle—a real one, not a peashooter like the one in your holster—and I know how to use it. Brought back plenty of pikhron skins to sell to old Porst, and he knows better than to try and cheat me. Why, I've even got a pack beast—all you've got to do is lend me the credits to rent a few pieces of gear that we'd need."

"Wouldn't we need more than one pack beast?" Luke asked.

Farnay looked away with a scowl.

"Mine will do," she muttered. "He's a bit small, but he's strong."

"I think I better see this pack beast of yours."

"Fine," Farnay said, and marched away, with Luke hurrying to catch up. She led him to a small house on the edge of the jungle. Outside, a leathery-skinned quadruped was tied to a stake. The beast raised its head, munching grass contentedly, and bleated at them.

"I am not programmed for zoology, but this animal appears to be a juvenile," Threepio said.

Luke sighed and rubbed the beast's nose, smiling as the animal closed its eyes and chuffed happily.

"I'm sure he's very strong, Farnay, but the two of us plus my droids would be too much for him to carry. You know that."

Farnay turned away, head down, and kicked at the dirt.

"But the information about Eedit's valuable," Luke

said, reaching into his jacket to give her some credits. "Let me—"

Farnay turned, already waving her hand dismissively, but whatever she'd planned to say died in her throat. Her eyes went wide, and Luke realized she'd seen the lightsaber under his jacket. Before he could say anything, she'd taken a step back and drawn a small but wicked-looking pistol from her tool belt.

"You touch that laser sword and I'll shoot you," she said. "And you'll get the same if you try to take over my brain. I've heard the stories, so don't try it."

Threepio let out a squawk of protest, and Luke raised his hands slowly, imagining his dreams coming to nothing because he'd frightened a teenage farm girl into shooting him.

"Farnay, take it easy," he said. "I'm not a Jedi—the lightsaber belonged to my father. He's dead—it's my only connection to him."

That was true, he thought sourly.

"What are you then?" Farnay demanded. "You're paying Dad a crazy amount of credits not to report your ship to the Empire. Are you some kind of rebel?"

"Master Korl is a hyperspace scout, as he told your father," Threepio said. "Don't you know it's rude to question your elders, young lady? To say nothing of pointing weapons at them."

Something was whispering in Luke's brain, offering

him reassurance—and telling him what to do.

"It's all right, Threepio. Farnay, put the gun down. We both know you're not going to shoot me."

"I will, too!"

Luke lowered his hands slowly and looked into Farnay's eyes.

"My real name is Luke Skywalker, and I *am* a rebel—I'm fighting to restore freedom to the galaxy."

"Oh dear, oh dear," Threepio said.

Farnay blinked at him, then lowered her pistol. Her hands were shaking.

"By getting rid of the Empire? But that would mean chaos . . . chaos and disorder."

"No, it wouldn't," Luke said. "It would mean peace and justice for everyone—instead of just a privileged few."

"You're crazy. Overthrowing the Empire is impossible."

"It's *not* impossible," Luke said, remembering how he'd used the Force to guide his proton torpedo to its target on the Death Star. "Sometimes it feels that way, I know. But people like me are working together on thousands of worlds to resist the Empire. And on thousands more worlds, people are realizing that the Empire's order comes at an enormous price—planets ruined and lives lost. All to feed the Emperor's greed."

Farnay looked off into the jungle.

"Before the war with the droids, when my parents were young, people in this town were farmers," she said. "They followed the old ways, living in harmony with the forest elders—that's what *pikhron* means in our language. Then the Empire came. Their governor wanted to go on a pikhron hunt, but no one would take him. So the Empire told us we couldn't send our crops to market—they left them to rot in the fields. It was lead the hunts or starve."

Luke nodded. It was a small cruelty compared with the crushing of freedom on so many worlds, not to mention the obliteration of Alderaan. But Luke knew the Empire wasn't just warships and stormtroopers. It was a billion small cruelties, grinding up what people cherished and leaving ruin and hopelessness behind.

"Now most of the villagers don't care about the old ways, and there aren't many pikhrons left in the jungle," Farnay said. "My father makes his living fixing the outlanders' starships—he won't serve as a guide."

"But you do," Luke said gently.

"My mother died last year," Farnay said, tears starting in her eyes. "I had to do something, or we would have lost our house. Dad was so angry with me, but what choice did I have? But it doesn't matter—no one hires me unless there isn't anybody else left. I've never bagged a pikhron."

"No skins, huh?"

"None," Farnay said, then smiled wanly. "I'm not sad about that part. But things will be different now, here in Tikaroo. That's why the rebels sent you here, isn't it? To help us."

"No," Luke said. "I wasn't sent here. I was . . . called. To the temple."

Farnay took a step back, looking wary. She slowly began to raise her blaster.

"Called? Called by what?"

"I don't know," Luke admitted. "It's . . . hard to explain. But I'm afraid my mission is there, not here."

Farnay turned away, head bowed in disappointment.

"But if you're patient, I promise I'll find a way to help Tikaroo," he said. "Somehow what I find in the temple will show me how to do that."

"I don't understand," Farnay said.

Luke smiled. He could almost feel the Force, humming around them, binding the jungle and its creatures together.

"Neither do I," Luke said. "Not yet. But I will."

CHAPTER 06

INTO THE WOODS

WHEN LUKE AND THREEPIO returned to the depot a lean alien was sitting in a chair on the porch, cleaning a long, boxy-looking blaster rifle. As the young rebel approached, the alien lifted his head—and Luke took a reflexive step backward.

He saw no visible eyes or mouth, just four segmented plates of chitin, the largest at the top. Small bristles lined the gaps between the plates, waving slightly. The rest of the alien's head was hidden beneath a battered old helmet of gray metal. Black tubes ran from the helmet's cheeks to a control box strapped to the alien's chest, tucked between bandoliers with bulging pockets. From the control box, two more tubes extended back over his shoulders.

The alien's forearms were covered with chitinous plates resembling the ones on his head, and studded with wispy hairs. He wore a torn cape over his left shoulder, and mismatched armor protected his left forearm and right shoulder.

Luke couldn't remember seeing an alien of his species before. He wondered what purpose the control box and tubes served. Were they breathing tubes? Did this species even breathe?

The alien finished inspecting the rifle and cocked his head at the two new arrivals. Despite his lack of eyes, Luke had the feeling he was being scrutinized—and not particularly favorably.

"You're Marcus—the outlander who wants to go on a pikhron hunt."

The words emerged from a vocoder grill at the helmet's chin. The voice was deep and low, like the rumble of an approaching storm.

"I'm not a hunter, but I want to hire a guide, yes. Are you available, Mr. . . . ?"

"Sarco Plank." The blank face seemed to regard Luke, and the cilia between the plates vibrated feverishly. "I'll take you into the jungle. For the right price."

Luke felt a strange current rippling in the Force.

"All of the other guides said no," he said. "Why are you different?"

"Because I don't listen to tall tales about ghosts and sorcerers. And because I have my own gear and mounts.

So there's nothing that old Porst can do about it."

That feeling in the Force was still there, like a bad taste in Luke's mouth. He didn't know if it was connected to Sarco, or something else. But even if it was a warning about Sarco, what could he do? Farnay's half-grown pack beast would never be able to take them, and no other guides were available. It was either go with Sarco or risk the journey on his own. And he had a rebel mission to get back to.

"Very well," Luke said, wondering if he was making a mistake—and if so, what price he would pay for it.

Two hours later, Luke came down from his room with the droids to find Sarco outside the depot with a pair of massive creatures. They had gray flesh, broad flat noses, and beady black eyes that were almost invisible in their wrinkled faces. Their forelegs were stubby, ending in broad feet, while the back legs were longer and powerful-looking.

Sarco cinched a howdah over one of the beast's shoulders and tightened it. The creature grunted in protest, and Sarco aimed a kick at its head, causing it to open a broad gash of a mouth filled with flat yellow teeth. It snapped at Sarco, stomping each foot in turn.

"We might as well be devoured right here," Threepio said mournfully, and Artoo let out an electronic moan.

"The happabores don't eat flesh," Sarco said. "Or metal. Just stay away from their mouths. And feet."

"That doesn't make me feel much safer," Threepio said.

"I'm sure it will be fine," Luke said, trying to conceal his own doubt. "Come on, Threepio, let's get you and Artoo saddled up."

He and Sarco struggled to get Threepio up onto the seat atop the smaller happabore, with the golden droid protesting mightily. Luke then tied Artoo on his side behind Threepio. He tugged on the ropes to make sure the astromech was secure, and Artoo hooted unhappily, rotating his dome to fix his single electronic eye reproachfully on Luke.

"I know you don't like it," Luke said, patting the droid's side. "I don't like it, either. We'll get you down from there as soon as possible."

As Sarco secured a pair of hunting rifles to the lead happabore's howdah, Farnay came charging around the corner of the depot. She stopped short, mouth a shocked O, and then balled her hands into fists.

"Uh-oh," Luke said.

"So it's true, then," she said. "I didn't want to believe it! You're actually going into the woods with the Scavenger!"

"You know I don't like that name," Sarco growled. "Or kids telling tales."

"Tales about what?" Farnay asked. "Your customers who don't come back?"

She turned to Luke, eyes pleading.

"He's a wicked creature—don't go with him! I'm begging you!"

"Perhaps it would be better if Artoo and I stayed here and supervised repairs," Threepio said.

Luke put his hands on Farnay's shoulders.

"I'll be careful," he said quietly. "Remember, I've got a trick or two up my sleeve."

"So does he," Farnay said. Tears started in her eyes and she wiped at them. Then she ran off.

"Time to go, Marcus," Sarco said, stepping on a stubby horn behind the happabore's eye and swinging himself up onto the howdah's forward seat.

Luke looked sadly in the direction Farnay had gone, then put his hands uncertainly on the happabore's shoulder. The gray flesh was thick and tough, but warm to the touch. Bracing himself, he clambered up onto the howdah's rear seat, his jacket flapping open as the structure swayed beneath them.

"I have a bad feeling about this," Threepio said as Sarco jabbed a prod into the side of the happabore's head and the huge beasts picked their way down the narrow path that led past the massive spire looming over Tikaroo and into the jungle.

————

It took a few minutes for Luke to get used to the jolting gait of the happabores and take a real look at the Devaronian jungle surrounding them. It was cool beneath the towering trees, with bird cries punctuating the rising and falling thrum of insects calling to one another. The happabores clambered over tangles of massive tree roots, their tiny eyes peering out at the trail ahead.

Artoo offered a quiet beep from his place atop the rear happabore.

"Peaceful?" Threepio snapped. "You're obviously malfunctioning. I expect that any moment we'll be stomped to bits. Or bitten in two by some monstrous predator."

"Or turned to scrap by a swarm of metal-eating bugs," Luke said with a grin. "Don't forget that one."

Sarco turned to regard the protocol droid. The chitinous plates of his head reminded Luke unsettlingly of overgrown toenails.

"Or blown to bits because you won't shut up," he said.

"Oh dear," Threepio said in a small voice.

"He's just kidding, Threepio," Luke said, then sensed something nearby. He peered into the jungle, trying to make sense of the rippling patterns of color and shade.

"Wait," he said, putting his hand on Sarco's shoulder. The alien shook it off, but tapped his mount with his prod. The happabore halted, its pinkish snout quivering, and gave a low moan that sounded like it was in pain.

"What is it, Marcus?" Sarco asked.

"I'm not sure. . . . It was a feeling I had."

Luke exhaled, trying to reach out not just with his senses, but also with his feelings.

"There," he said, pointing deeper into the jungle.

Through a stand of trees he saw four gray shapes, dappled in shadow. One moved slightly, and the shapes resolved themselves into sturdy legs, broad backs, and stubby heads crowned with curling horns.

They weren't happabores but rather the creatures Luke had seen in his vision. They'd stood nearby while he faced the three remotes with his lightsaber.

"Pikhrons," Sarco grunted. "You have keen senses for an outlander."

He handed one of the long-barreled blaster rifles to Luke, then raised his own bulky weapon.

"No," Luke said, pushing Sarco's rifle down.

"What? Why not?"

Luke shook his head. He realized he could feel the pikhrons in the Force—the comfort they took in one another and the pleasure they felt in the shade of their glen. He could also feel their wariness about the intruders atop the happabores and their urge to flee, which was warring with their instinct to remain still and silent.

"You're taking away a good payday, outlander," Sarco objected.

"I'll pay you whatever you would have earned from the skins," Luke said. "But we're leaving the pikhrons alone."

Sarco shrugged, returned the rifles to their slings, and jabbed the happabore with the prod. As the beasts resumed their journey through the jungle, Luke looked back to see the pikhrons ambling away through the trees.

"Did you grow up in these woods?" he asked Sarco.

"In Tikaroo," Sarco said. "This is home now. I only go into town when it's necessary. They don't like me there. They never have."

"I'm sorry."

Sarco just grunted.

"Mr. Sarco?" Threepio piped up. "Why do they call you the Scavenger? It seems a most peculiar name."

Luke grimaced. Sometimes he suspected whoever programmed Threepio for etiquette had installed something upside down.

"It's supposed to be an insult," Sarco said. "My

specialty is finding things of value and figuring out who wants them."

"If you grew up in Tikaroo, you must remember the days before the hunts," Luke said. "When the villagers followed the old ways."

The bristles on Sarco's arms quivered briefly.

"The old ways were sentimental nonsense. Animals are a resource, like everything else in the galaxy."

"But the people here lived in harmony with the pikhrons for generations."

Sarco shrugged.

"Besides, resources can be used up if we're not careful," Luke said.

"An entire galaxy's worth? Impossible. What's the point of caring about a few pikhrons? Or Devaron? Or any of it?"

Luke looked sadly at the stately trees, wondering what had happened to Sarco that he cared so little for his surroundings. He couldn't have been born that way—no one was. Something had warped and twisted him, turned him bitter and withdrawn.

"Besides," the alien muttered, "it's a better life traveling the jungle taking what you need than scratching at dirt with a plow."

"Now *that* I agree with," Luke said. "I grew up farming, myself. It's hard work."

Sarco turned his eyeless mask of chitin toward Luke. His cilia fluttered and he cocked his head to the left, then to the right.

"Thought you were a hyperspace scout," he said. "Isn't that your fighter that Kivas is working on?"

"That's right."

"You're a busy young man. Y-wing, eh? If you want to sell, I know people who'll pay good credits."

"What kind of people?" Luke asked.

Sarco shrugged.

"I find things," he said. "As long as people pay good credits, what they do with those things isn't my business."

"Well, my ship isn't for sale."

"What about the droid, then?"

"Of all the nerve!" Threepio exclaimed. "I am most certainly *not* for sale. Isn't that right, Master—"

"I meant the astromech," Sarco said. "You talk too much—nobody would buy you."

Artoo chortled and Luke had to smile.

"They're not for sale, either," he said. "But I've got a way you can make some easy credits. Take me to Eedit."

"Forbidden."

Artoo blatted derisively, and Sarco turned in his seat.

"What did it say?"

Threepio inclined his head haughtily.

"He said he thought you didn't believe in ghosts."

"You should shut those droids off," Sarco said.

"I was thinking the same thing as Artoo," Luke said. "What are you afraid of?"

"Nothing," Sarco said. "But there's a difference between brave and stupid. Ghosts aren't the danger at Eedit."

"What is, then?" Luke asked. "Look, I just want to see the place—I won't go inside. I'm . . . interested in old sites."

Sarco turned to regard Luke.

"First you're a hyperspace scout, now you're some kind of historian. Is that why you carry that antique laser sword? Out of historical interest?"

Luke hesitated, wondering when Sarco had detected his lightsaber. He cursed himself for not being more careful.

"Yes," he said. "That's it exactly. I'm interested in old sites, and relics."

"So am I," Sarco said, then cocked his head left and right. "So you carry a Jedi weapon, but you can't use it."

Luke forced himself to choke back his pride.

"It's still a useful tool," he said. "And before you ask, no, it's not for sale."

Sarco's cilia quivered in a way that made Luke uneasy. But then the alien turned away.

"Very well, Marcus," he said. "I'll take you to the barrier. For an additional price, of course."

CHAPTER 07
THE LOST TEMPLE

SARCO BROUGHT the happabores to a halt a few meters away from the edge of the jungle. He and Luke dismounted and peered out across a plateau dotted with copses of towering trees and overgrown with vines as thick around as Luke's leg. A stone road, cracked and almost entirely reclaimed by vegetation, led across the plateau to the shattered towers that Luke had seen from the air.

"No closer," Sarco warned, pointing ahead of them.

Luke noticed white spines sticking up from the ground. They were sensors, he realized—and they stretched in a perimeter between the edge of the jungle and the temple.

His heart sank. There was no way he could reach the temple without being detected.

Artoo whistled for their attention.

"Artoo says he's willing to deactivate the sensors," Threepio said. "Though that strikes me as reckless even by his standards."

"I'm afraid you're right," Luke said. "It's too risky—and we can't afford to get caught."

Sarco cocked his head at Luke, then turned his head so the chitinous mask faced the droids.

"I can take you somewhere else," he said, his electronically modulated voice curiously soft. "A place reserved for my best customers."

"What's there?"

Sarco cocked his head one way, then the other.

"It's a secret."

An image flashed into Luke's mind—a gloomy depression carpeted with moss, the jagged ends of old bones sticking out of the dirt and leaves.

Luke shook his head and took a step away from Sarco, his fingers creeping toward his lightsaber.

"I'm not interested in your secrets," he said firmly. "Is there any spot that gets us closer to the temple?"

Sarco's cilia fluttered and he waved his hands at the ring of Imperial sensors.

"Are you blind, boy? You can see for yourself that there's no way in."

"The lake, then," Luke said, thinking back to his vision of swimming beneath the Devaronian moons. "The one that's nearby."

Sarco stood stock-still for a moment, and Luke thought the alien seemed puzzled.

"There's no lake near here. Just the river and the old dam destroyed in the droid war. But there's nothing there—the valuable equipment was picked over long ago."

A dam? Luke thought, then realized what he'd seen in his dream wasn't a lake at all, but an artificial reservoir.

"The old dam? Is it outside the sensor barrier?"

"Yes. But I told you, outlander—there's nothing there."

"We'll see about that," Luke said.

The river had shrunk to a knee-deep channel meandering down the center of a bowl-shaped valley strewn with rock—Sarco said most of the water had been diverted for projects upstream. Even Threepio managed to cross with only a moderate amount of complaining.

Luke stared at the cliffs on the far side of the valley, looking for something he recognized from his vision, while Sarco kicked at the rocks. The old riverbed was littered with rusted droid parts and broken pieces of armor that had once been white but had turned a sickly yellow from years of exposure to the sun.

"Garbage," Sarco muttered, stooping to pick up the

angular head of a droid. "Nothing worth taking."

He flung the head through the air to land at Threepio's feet. The protocol droid peered down at it, and Artoo whistled.

"Switch heads?" Threepio asked. "What an unpleasant idea. Artoo-Detoo, some of the fantasies rattling around inside your dome border on the bizarre."

Artoo's only reply was a smug tootle.

Luke scanned the cliffs above until he could see the remnants of the braces that had once held the dam in place. They were little more than twisted wreckage now, but they told him where the top of the dam had been—and indeed, he could see a dark line on the rock that indicated the old waterline.

He looked below that line, telling himself to relax, to use the Force to direct his eyes.

There.

"Do you have macrobinoculars?" Luke asked hesitantly, thinking it was a ridiculous question to ask an alien who didn't have eyes.

A burst of static that Luke decided was laughter emerged from Sarco's vocoder. The alien opened a pouch on his bandolier and handed over a small but expensive pair of macrobinoculars.

"For customers," he explained.

Luke nodded, then focused in on the spot he'd seen and grinned.

"There's a cave up there," he said. "Maybe a kilo-meter upriver. It's about ten meters above the valley floor."

Sarco turned to face that way, then cocked his head at Luke.

"Your species can barely see the cave even with amplification. How did you know it was there?"

"I had a feeling it would be," Luke said, not wanting to explain further.

Sarco cocked his head left, then right.

"Impressive," he said. "But can you get up to it?"

"I think so," Luke said, eyes already tracing a way up the cliff.

Half an hour later he scrambled into the damp, cool cave, having come close to plummeting down the cliff face only once. He activated his lightsaber, the brilliant blue blade emerging from its hilt with a familiar snap and hiss.

Luke closed his eyes, enjoying the weight of the hilt in his hand. Then he opened them and held up his father's weapon, illuminating the walls of the cave. As in his vision, stone steps led up into the gloom. He followed them, thinking it was strange to find himself familiar with a place he'd never been.

The stairs ended at the spot where the alien Jedi's comrade had handed him his lightsaber. After a few meters the tunnel curved sharply to the right. Luke feared it would end in a solid wall, or a tumble of impassable rock, and thought about how discouraging it would be to have to ride back through the jungle with Sarco.

Don't center on your anxieties, he reminded himself, and peered around the corner.

The tunnel ran straight through the rock, as far as the illumination of his lightsaber reached. He tried to estimate which direction the tunnel headed, then stopped. He already knew where it led—straight into the Temple of Eedit. He knew because the Force was tugging at him, its message blessedly clear. This was what it had wanted him to find.

Getting the droids up the cliff took the better part of an hour and required haggling with Sarco over the use of his block and tackle. The alien had brought the equipment for hoisting a dead pikhron so the beast could be skinned; Luke was glad to use it for some other purpose.

Artoo suffered being hauled up to the cave with his dignity relatively intact, beeping encouragingly at Luke each time he caught his breath and fantasized about being able to lift the droids through the air using the Force. But Threepio spent the entire time declaring that the rope was slipping and predicting his imminent demise. With the protocol droid standing safely in the cave and marveling at his miraculous survival, Luke lowered Sarco's equipment and then tossed the rope down to him.

"We'll be inside for a few days at least," Luke called down to Sarco. "I'll raise you on the comlink when we're ready to return."

Sarco raised his head from where he stood in the riverbed, arranging his equipment on his shoulders.

"If you come out of there alive," he said.

Luke hesitated. He didn't believe in ghosts, but Ben had warned him about the power of the dark side of the Force—it had corrupted his apprentice Darth Vader. What if it was behind the stories of spirits in the temple? What if some malevolent energy still lingered there?

"I can take care of myself," he told Sarco, scanning the forested cliffs across the river. For a moment he thought he'd seen something glinting in the sun.

"You'll get more credits, if that's what you're worrying about," he added.

I'm running up quite a bill for the Alliance, he thought wryly. *I better learn to use the Force to trick a quartermaster into approving it.*

Sarco cocked his head back and forth in that strange, vaguely clockwork habit he had.

"We'll meet again, Marcus," he said, and strode off across the rocky valley to where the happabores were waiting.

"What an unpleasant creature," sniffed Threepio.

"I kind of feel sorry for him," Luke said. "But look, he got us this far, didn't he?"

"Wherever that may be."

"Right," Luke said. "That's a good question. Let's find out the answer."

They walked for longer than half an hour, footsteps echoing in the close confines of the tunnel, while Threepio imagined various calamities that were certain to befall them.

As they walked, a sense of calm settled over Luke. His father's lightsaber felt like an extension of his hand, and his senses were quick to register each chip and divot in the tunnel, each slight current of air. He was aware of his breathing in and out, and of the unhurried beat of his heart.

It's the Force, he realized. *It's getting stronger. Stronger, or perhaps I'm feeling a deeper connection with it.*

Something gleamed in the pale blue light of his saber. Luke held up his hand for the droids to stop, interrupting Threepio's speech about what it would be like to be entombed for millennia without power while vermin chewed through his wiring.

There were pieces of stone scattered across the floor. Beyond them, the passageway sloped upward but was blocked by fallen rocks. Luke advanced cautiously, clambering up the pile and peering through the tumbled stones.

"Oh no, it's obviously completely impassable," Threepio said. "I suppose we'll have to go back to Tikaroo."

"No, it's mostly loose stone," Luke said. "I can feel fresh air, in fact. Come and help me clear this stuff out of the way."

"But, Master Luke, I'm not programmed for demolition."

"Neither am I. We'll just have to do our best."

Artoo hooted at Threepio and rolled to the edge of the pile. He extended a utility arm and plucked a small stone out of the tumble, then turned and rolled away with his prize, whistling cheerfully.

"Well, that's no end of help," Threepio said.

Together they shoved the loose rock aside, Luke carving away at some of the bigger blocks with his saber, careful not to let the liquefied rock burn him. He found himself whistling a sprightly tune as he worked.

"Master Luke!" Threepio exclaimed. "That sound you're making—it's the first Whiforlan fluting form!"

"Is it?" Luke asked, smiling. "It's catchy."

Luke climbed to the top of the pile, pushed at a slab of stone with his shoulder, and was rewarded when it slid aside and then toppled out of sight, landing with a crash.

"We're almost there," he said. "If we get the big pieces moved you and Artoo should be able to get through."

He pushed his head through the gap he'd created, then his shoulders, saber raised to illuminate his surroundings. What he saw made his heart catch in his throat.

"I'm going to take a quick look around," Luke said. "I'll be back in a couple of minutes."

"Be careful, Master Luke!" Threepio said.

Luke scrambled through the gap and found himself on the edge of what once had been an enormous hall, lit by the light of late afternoon.

Much of the roof had tumbled down, columns were shorn off or toppled, and the floor was covered with drifts of leaves that had blown in through shattered windows. The center of the floor was a crater, surrounded by rubble. Something screeched in the shadows, the noise of its scrambling retreat echoing around Luke. He whirled in a circle, brandishing his father's lightsaber in front of him, then forced himself to take a deep breath.

It's not a demon or dark-side ghosts—just jungle creatures, he thought. *You've invaded their home, that's all.*

He raised his saber high and saw two statues at the far end of the hall, their faces bubbled and blackened, their arms ending in cauterized stumps. The temple had been bombed and then vandalized with heavy energy weapons—someone had worked hard to erase any sign of beauty that had escaped the initial spasm of violence.

The Empire, Luke thought. *The purpose of the attack was to ruin this place and eradicate what it stood for. What it meant to people.*

He felt his anger rise—anger for the people of Alderaan, for his aunt and uncle on Tatooine, for his father, and for so many millions of others.

He nearly tripped over the stone hand on the floor. It had come to lie on its side, atop a pile of rubble. The wrist was blackened where it had been sheared away, but the hand itself was intact, as if stretched out toward him in welcome. The stonework was beautiful, he thought, running his hand over the fingers, appreciating the detail some lost artisan had created over untold hours. His eyes jumped to the statues looming above, and he saw where the hand had been attached.

Luke deactivated his lightsaber and hung it on his belt. He pushed the stone hand aside and sifted through the rubble beneath it. Here was the upper part of a face, with an eye captured in swift, confident strokes, the eyebrow arched in good humor. There was a chin, bearded, and above it a smile.

His anger drained from him, to be replaced by a quiet joy. The Empire had tried to erase everything that had been beautiful there, but it had failed. He could still see that beauty, just as he could feel the power of the Force surrounding him.

At the end of the grand hall, the remains of massive double doors hung from their hinges. The entrance was filled with rubble higher than Luke's head, and the wind had mounded up leaves in the corners. He started toward the doors, then decided against it—the Empire might have other safeguards against intrusion, in addition to the perimeter sensors. He turned the other way instead, passing corridors choked with wreckage, and found a series of arches leading to an open space overgrown with trees.

Luke squeezed between two tumbled slabs and found himself in a circular courtyard created from the space between the two ruined towers and the rubble of smaller buildings that had been part of the temple complex. Once manicured, the courtyard was now wild. Impact craters had opened yawning pits in the ground, through which Luke could barely make out tumbled stone in the gloom far below. The bowl of a ruined fountain occupied the center of the space, with water bubbling up from inside and spilling out over flagstones covered with grass, forming a shallow pool. Faceless, limbless statues, much smaller than the ones in the great hall, formed a perimeter around the fountain.

Luke looked around in mingled disbelief and joy. It was the place he'd seen in his vision—the fountain, the statues, the grass and trees. Somehow its disheveled state made it even lovelier than he imagined it had been when carefully groomed and tended.

Something made a low sound nearby, and Luke saw pikhrons standing quietly among the trees on the far side of the courtyard, watching him warily. An old matriarch tossed her head, and the group pushed its way through the trees, peering at Luke with small black eyes. They climbed a low mound of rubble, all that remained of one wing of the temple, and were gone.

They feel safe here, Luke thought. *They know the hunters don't come inside the perimeter.*

"Luke . . ."

Luke turned in surprise, looking for the source of the voice he'd heard.

"This place is strong with the Force," Ben Kenobi said in Luke's head. "It was the will of the Force that guided you to this place. Here you will learn to open yourself to the Force, guiding its possibilities and obeying its commands. And passing its tests. May the Force be with you, Luke."

"Ben!" Luke called, but the voice of his old teacher was silent.

Luke sat down on the rim of the fountain, in one of the long shadows the statues cast across the glen. He could feel the power around him—power and a sense of peace. This was the place the Force had shown him, and where it had brought him.

"Master Luke?"

That voice hadn't been in his head. Luke looked up and saw Threepio and Artoo standing in one of the archways to the great hall.

"Over here, Threepio."

"There you are! Master Luke, we've found something."

"What have you found?"

Artoo let out a torrent of accusatory beeps.

"Oh, very well, *you* found it," Threepio said. "Artoo found a damaged frieze—apparently without *my* help—and we thought it might be of interest."

"Let's see what you've got," Luke said, following the droids back into the ruined hall, to a section in deep shadow.

Artoo activated a spotlight on his dome and traced it along the wall. Luke leaned forward, hands on his knees. The sculpted figures on the wall were as damaged as the statues, the scenes interrupted by craters left by blaster fire. But Luke could make out children in Jedi robes, lightsabers raised in front of them as an instructor demonstrated the proper defensive stance.

Farther down the wall, Luke saw fragments of scenes in which Jedi fought warriors wearing spiked armor and masks. Even frozen in stone, the Jedi looked like deadly dancers, captured in the act of leaping and tumbling, their lightsabers like extensions of their bodies.

I'll never be able to do that—I can barely fend off an attack from a training remote. I wouldn't even know how to learn *to do that. So much knowledge has been lost. No, not lost—stolen from the galaxy. Stolen by Vader and the Emperor.*

The frieze ended in shattered stone, and Artoo shut off his light.

"I'm glad I got to see that," Luke said. "But everything here took place a long time ago. This place is important because of the present, not the past. The Force told me so."

He returned to the glade, which was filled with birdsong, and looked around the courtyard again. His gaze lingered on a stone pillar whose surface was broken by a lever extending from the stone two-thirds of the way to the top, meters above his head.

"Unless the Jedi who lived here were very tall, that was designed to be opened with the Force," he said.

Luke unbuckled his belt and holster and set it down on a tumbled slab of rock next to the droids. Holding his deactivated lightsaber in one hand, he walked over and stood beneath the pillar, its surface turned orange by the setting sun. He breathed deeply, tuning out the squabbling droids and pushing away the distracting thoughts crowding his head.

Keep your concentration here and now.

He reached out with his hand, imagining it gripping the lever and pulling.

Nothing happened.

Luke shook his head and tried again, ordering the lever to move, then conjuring a picture of the Force taking on the form of something that could pull it. He closed his eyes and tried to imagine it was only him and the lever he was trying to move. When he looked again, the lever would have shifted and the pedestal would be open.

Luke opened his eyes. Nothing had changed.

He wiped his brow on his sleeve, took a deep breath, and tried again.

And then again. And again and again and again.

Luke tried until the glade was shrouded in gloom, with only the tops of the ruined towers still painted in the colors of sunset. The birds had stilled their songs and sought their nests. But the lever still hadn't moved. No matter what he did, the Force refused to obey his commands—or his pleas.

I can't do it. I don't understand how, and there's no one to teach me. And there never will be—I'm the last of the Jedi.

The last of the Jedi sank to the grass in despair.

Farnay had watched through her macrobinoculars as Luke disappeared into the cave, gasping when he seemed to look straight at her for a moment. She'd observed Sarco as he trudged back across the rocky valley and scrambled up to where his beasts waited.

She was about a hundred meters away from him, crouched behind a thick tree trunk, her pack beast staked nearby.

She expected Sarco to climb atop one of the mounts and start back toward Tikaroo. But instead the faceless alien set up a campsite not far from the edge of the cliff, across the river valley from the cave.

He's waiting, Farnay thought. *Waiting for Luke.*

Farnay knew better than to think the Scavenger was waiting in case he might be of help. She knew what he really wanted—a chance to loot the sorcerers' temple without attracting Imperial attention. And Luke's presence wouldn't be enough to dissuade him. The Scavenger's customers had a way of meeting accidents in the jungle. Most of the missing were wealthy but eccentric old hunters without people who would report them as missing or come looking for them.

She didn't know what had happened to them, but she could guess. And if the Scavenger decided Luke was in his way, it would happen to him, too.

CHAPTER 08
THE LIVING FORCE

I N THE MORNING Luke awoke from a deep, dreamless sleep.

He looked around the glade, momentarily confused, before he remembered where he was. When he sat up Artoo turned his radar eye in his master's direction, beeping a cheery good morning, then rocked sideways to bump Threepio's silver knee. The protocol droid gave a startled hop as his photoreceptors lit up.

Luke ate a ration bar, drank some cool, clean water from the fountain, and stood in the dew-speckled grass, staring up at the pillar again.

I was exhausted yesterday, but I'm rested now. The Force will obey me more easily.

He sighed and reached up toward the lever with an open hand, letting his shoulders rise and fall.

Nothing happened.

He tried for longer than an hour, as the morning sun evaporated the dew from the grass and the birds began to zip through the branches. Discouraged, he forced himself to sit against the stone bowl of the old fountain and meditate until he had chased away his negative thoughts. Then he got up, walked over to the pillar, and told the lever to move.

It remained still.

Luke kicked a loose flagstone across the glade, startling a crowd of brilliant green birds, then hopped across the glade with his injured toe in hand.

"I'm fine," he said before Threepio could suggest that it was only sensible to summon a rebel medical frigate immediately.

Luke stretched out his hand, then pulled it back as a buzzing insect landed on his wrist. He shooed it away, annoyed, but it landed again, its crystalline wings catching the early-morning light. One compound eye swiveled to regard him as the insect picked its way along his wrist, its coiled proboscis darting out to taste the sweat on his skin.

"I'm not a flower," Luke said. "Buzz off."

The sap drinker ignored him. Its feet tickled. Luke looked at its teardrop-shaped body, a graceful curve that ended in a barbed stinger. He knew it wouldn't sting him—that was a defense against creatures that might attack its nest. Luke held up his wrist, admiring the way the little creature's iridescent blue body shimmered when seen from different angles. He smiled at the exuberant life contained in that tiny, busy living thing.

"To harness the Force, you must first feel it everywhere," said the voice of Ben Kenobi.

Luke frowned, then reached out with his senses. He could feel the Force inside himself, a bright shining thing bubbling and roiling. He reached for the sap drinker still exploring his wrist, not with his hand but with his feelings. There it was—a point of light in the Force, tiny but brilliant. The sap drinker's presence seemed to overlap with his own body, his own presence in the Force.

The sap drinker flew away with a whir of wings. Luke tried to track its presence in the Force, but the chaotic ripples in the glade were too confusing. There seemed to be millions of currents around him, all emanating from living things—birds and insects, but also the leaves of the trees and the tiny unseen creatures borne on the wind or scuttling across bark and rock. All those lives were vessels of the Force, containers for its energy.

Luke tried to find the sap drinker's presence again amid the tumult, then stopped.

Trying to focus on a single living thing was confusing and exhausting. But the Force wasn't limited to those individual bodies, he realized. They created the Force and made it grow, but it escaped those boundaries, overflowing them just like the spring escaped the broken rim of the fountain.

Luke closed his eyes and let himself sink into the Force, allowing it to wash over him. He let his awareness drift, carried this way and that by the living presences around him and the way they made the energy field ripple and dance. He could feel the Force radiating out from his own body, just as it spilled from the birds and insects and tiny creatures.

New ripples passed over him, and he could feel bright presences nearby. Luke opened his eyes and saw the pikhrons clambering over the rubble of the fallen temple wing. They sniffed at him, then lowered their heads and began to graze.

Luke smiled and reached through the Force again, but this time he wasn't trying to push the energy field across an empty space—he was swimming through it, meandering across the currents of energy in the glade. He traced the rock of the pillar by the way the Force surrounded it—the rock wasn't alive, but it was an emptiness defined by the life covering it. He could feel the ridges and crannies, the cracks that offered refuge to microscopic living things. He felt the pillar's shape as his awareness climbed it and found the lever.

Luke bent his wrist and the lever moved as easily as if he'd held it in his hand.

The compartment inside the pillar contained a dozen training remotes, all covered with moss from their long years in damp confinement. Most of them refused to come back to life, either damaged by moisture or having lost all their charge. But Luke and Artoo managed to get three of them working, scrubbing them free of moss and dirt before closing up their access ports.

"Master Luke, are you sure that's a good idea?" Threepio asked. "They could be an Imperial trap designed to kill intruders. Shouldn't you at least have your pistol ready just in case?"

"I'll risk it," Luke said with a smile.

He stepped back from the remotes, and they rose into the air, rotating slowly so their sensors could evaluate their surroundings. Artoo turned to roll away, and one of the remotes charged him, retreating hastily when the little droid screeched at it indignantly. After zipping about for a few seconds, two of the remotes returned to the pillar, hovering in front of it for a few seconds and then touching down inside the compartment. The third remote floated in front of Luke, as if waiting for something.

Ben's voice filled Luke's head again.

"The lightsaber disciplines the mind and schools the body and spirit," he said. "Mind what you have learned. Let the lightsaber be your focus."

Luke nodded and detached his father's weapon from his belt. He spread his feet wide, ignited the lightsaber, and swung it around one-handed in a loose arc. Then he took hold of it with both hands.

The remote floated before him, turning lazily in the air. It zipped to one side, then the other, and Luke had the distinct feeling the device was sizing him up as an opponent.

"Be careful, Master Luke," Threepio urged.

Feel the Force, Luke reminded himself. *It will give you the reflexes you need to guide the blade where it needs to be.*

Luke remembered the first time he'd ever held his father's lightsaber, in Ben's little stone house on the edge of the Dune Sea. He remembered how the brilliant blue-white blade had dazzled his eyes and then seemed to draw them in, and the almost hypnotic sound of the blade. And he remembered how even though he'd never seen a lightsaber, let alone held one, the weapon had instantly felt right in his hand.

Ben had told him to hold the grip so the blade would be high and ready when it appeared. He'd shown him that everything you could do with a lightsaber—attack, defend, advance, withdraw—began with the initial stance. Dominant foot back, blade held in parry position on the dominant side. Feet not too wide, the better for speed and agility.

Luke assumed the position, watching the remote as it eased back and forth in front of him, its movements deceptively slow. He wondered if it had a way of sensing his ability, or if different remotes were programmed for different levels of skill. What if the remotes used to train raw apprentices were all damaged and the Force had brought him there to be peppered with laser bolts that only advanced students could have swatted away?

The remote dove to the right and zipped at Luke's head. He dodged instinctively, raising the blade high and keeping it between him and his attacker.

First defensive posture, he remembered. *Now pay attention. You can worry about programming remotes later.*

The remote returned to its initial position in front of the pillar, with Luke turning to face it. Then his blade was diving down and to his right, to protect his hip. The remote's laser blast struck the blade, sending tendrils of energy snaking across it, and then dissipated in the morning air.

That was the second defensive posture.

Threepio raised his hands in celebration.

"You did it, Master Luke!"

Somehow Han's mocking laughter at his getting zapped by a laser blast aboard the *Falcon* had been less annoying than Threepio's congratulations.

Luke smiled at the thought, then had to dodge left in response to the remote's feint, holding the blade in the third defensive posture. He glanced quickly at the pits gouged in the glade, marking their position. It wouldn't do to tumble into the depths.

The remote weaved to the right, then darted behind him. Luke whirled, blade high, and a bolt of energy shot by his head to sizzle in the damp grass. The remote retreated, and Luke brought his lightsaber back to the ready position.

"Excellent, Master Luke," Threepio called.

"Not really—I should have deflected it," Luke said. "I got lucky."

That attack forced me into the fourth defensive posture, he thought. *The remote ran through all four basic defensive forms in order. It's testing what I've learned.*

Which meant it would now attack him for real.

The remote floated in front of him, its jets hissing faintly as it moved up and down, then left and right. It dodged left, but Luke was already bringing his blade down to the right, even as the remote reversed course and fired at his knee. Luke deflected the laser bolt, then wheeled his blade the other way, sending energy beams flying back the way they'd come.

This time the remote didn't back off but accelerated, following a zigzag course and peppering him with fire. Luke's blade was a blue blur, deflecting bolts all around him. He slipped slightly as he tried to return to ready position, then leapt over a flurry of bolts aimed at his feet.

Luke's mind flashed back to the Mos Eisley cantina, where two alien thugs had picked a fight with him. Ben had tried to play peacemaker, sensing Luke's growing panic, but the aliens hadn't been interested in peace. One had flung Luke into a table, then gone for his blaster, ready to gun Ben down.

The old Jedi's hand had dipped to the lightsaber on his belt, faster than anyone would have imagined a desert hermit could move. His lightsaber sliced the blaster aimed at him in two, then carved through the thugs.

It was the first time Luke had ever seen a lightsaber in action, and what amazed him was that there was no wasted motion—one moment two alien bullies were threatening an old man's life, and the next moment their days of threatening anyone were over.

Ben had stood for a moment, coolly regarding the other patrons at the bar with the lightsaber held before him in ready position. Then he'd deactivated his blade and helped Luke up from where he'd been sprawled on the filthy floor, looking on in awe.

Luke tried to imagine what the patrons of the cantina had thought to see a Jedi Knight in their midst after nearly two decades in which Force-users had been nothing more than rumor and legend. What had it been like when Jedi were common sights in the galaxy? And would such a day ever come again?

The remote zipped left, then right, then cut back to the left and shot Luke in the knee. He yelped at the sting of the laser bolt as the machine returned to floating in front of him.

"Artoo! That dreadful machine has injured Master Luke!"

"Just my pride," Luke said, wiping the sweat from his forehead and reminding himself to quit daydreaming.

When he resumed the ready position the remote began to dart from side to side again, testing his defenses. It tried to get behind him, and he parried the pencil-thin shaft of laser light, sending it caroming off an annoyed Artoo. He kept turning as the remote dove at his feet, leaping over its bolts and reminding himself to keep his guard up.

Luke took two more hits and lowered his blade, causing the remote to back away. He told himself to ignore Threepio's comments and push out the fear of failure trying to creep into his head.

Ben had been gentle after the death of Uncle Owen and Aunt Beru, letting Luke grieve for his family and rage at the Empire for murdering them. His emotions were natural, Ben said, and his love for his family did him credit. But he then warned that Luke must resist the desire for revenge. Anger and hatred could help him draw power from the Force—but only at a terrible price. For those emotions unlocked the dark side of the Force, leading a Jedi to temptation—and sometimes ruin.

A Jedi had to learn to let go of anger before calling on the Force, Ben had instructed. But he or she also had to let go of fear—for fear led to anger, inviting the dark side in.

"I'm not afraid," Luke said, raising his saber again. "I won't fail."

The remote tried to zip around behind him. He whirled, blade humming, and blocked its shot—then turned the other way as it tried to reverse course and target his hip. He deflected a shot aimed at his head, then one intended for his knee, then leapt to avoid one that struck at his feet. He smiled to himself but then pushed the elation away, too, trying to see and hear nothing but the remote.

It felt like he and the remote were dancing, like they were somehow connected—man and machine, joined by the energy of the training laser and the blade of Luke's lightsaber. They moved together—first for a minute, then for five, and then Luke lost all track of time.

When the remote backed away he didn't register it at first but simply waited, barely conscious that he was breathing hard. Then he realized the remote had stopped attacking and lowered his blade, letting his shoulders slump.

"Well done, Master Luke!" Threepio called. "A most impressive display!"

Luke smiled at the protocol droid, waving to acknowledge Artoo's enthusiastic whistles. Then the remote chattered in an electronic language and a second remote rose to float alongside it.

Luke's smile faded away.

PART
THREE

CHAPTER 09
THE WEAPON OF A JEDI KNIGHT

LUKE KNEW THE TWO REMOTES wouldn't attack until he raised his lightsaber to ready position, so he took a moment to catch his breath. Then he nodded and lifted his arms, blade held out in front of him.

As he'd expected, the two remotes drifted apart, taking up positions on either side of him. One after another they darted in, forcing him to reorient his defenses. Then they retreated. Luke felt his heartbeat quickening as he tried to watch both of them, his feet automatically carrying him backward so he'd have a better chance of keeping them both in sight.

The remotes followed him.

Don't fall in a pit, Luke reminded himself.

One of the remotes dove at his left. A quarter second later, the other remote attacked him from the right. Luke had expected that and brought his saber sweeping around in an overhead arc, the blade intersecting the laser blast.

Which was when the other remote hit him in the seat of his pants.

"Ow," Luke complained, fighting the urge to rub the spot as the remotes retreated.

They swooped in again, and this time Luke blocked three shots before the remote to his right slipped a shot through his guard, leaving his knee numb.

Luke shook the tingling out of his leg and raised his saber again.

He was so busy worrying about how to tell the difference between an attack and a feint that the left-hand remote's very first shot hit him in the wrist.

"Stop," Luke said, sitting down in the grass with a sigh of disgust. The remotes backed off, hovering around waist level.

"You're right to quit, Master Luke," Threepio said. "Two against one is hardly sporting."

"I'm not quitting," Luke insisted. "I'm just resting for a moment."

I had it, he thought. *I was commanding the Force. I barely noticed time was passing.*

But that had been against one opponent, not two. This was twice as hard—and completely different.

You can do this, Luke told himself, getting to his feet.

Ben had only had a brief period of time to teach him how to wield his father's lightsaber—a few lessons aboard the *Falcon* in which Luke had learned the basic defensive postures and the first steps in opening himself to the Force. But since then he'd practiced the footwork more times than he could count, striving to recall every moment of the time he'd had with his teacher. And those movements had become second nature. He'd come so far since his first tentative practice session aboard the *Falcon*.

He raised his saber, reminding himself to be light on his feet.

He blocked shots from either side, then stumbled trying to dodge the next one. He rolled over, his saber scorching grass and flagstones, and bounded up with his blade held out in front of him. The remotes circled, trying to break through his defenses.

The remotes both charged him from the right—but one went high and one went low. Luke deflected the bolt the raised remote aimed at his shoulder, but the other one caught him in the knee.

Luke lowered his saber, grimacing. He'd moved with speed and grace, but that wasn't enough. He'd been foolish to think it could be. He couldn't track two remotes at once—it was hard enough keeping up with one.

You can do it if you draw on the Force, he thought, and raised the saber again.

He caught one remote's bolt on his blade, sending it into the glade and scattering a rainbow of protesting songbirds. The other remote fired a bolt past his head, then zipped left and took aim at him again. He deflected the bolt into the grass at his feet, cleaving down with the saber to intercept a shot from the first remote. Then he snapped back to ready position, waving his saber back and forth.

He fought until the sun was low in the sky and the pikhrons were pale shapes in the gloom. One of the remotes swooped down at him and he deflected its bolt straight back at it, enveloping the little machine in sparks. It retreated and beeped accusingly at him.

"About time you got a taste of your own medicine," said Threepio.

Then a third remote rose out of the compartment in the pillar.

Luke put his hands on his knees, breathing hard, then deactivated his father's weapon. His arms were shaking with fatigue.

"That's enough for today," he said, and after a minute of uncertain hovering the remotes retreated to their compartment and shut themselves down.

All Luke wanted to do was sleep, but he forced himself to bathe as best he could in the fountain and then activate the warming unit on a tin of food concentrate.

Threepio had set up the portable heater, and Luke settled himself gratefully in front of its glow, poking at his dinner.

The droids sat on the other side of the heater, sharing a recharge from the portable battery Luke had brought. Beyond them the pikhrons lowed quietly to one another.

"I must say, your exercises are stimulating to observe, Master Luke," Threepio said. "Your agility has improved immensely. No doubt that's thanks to watching the recordings Artoo and I discovered."

"No doubt," Luke said.

Artoo let out an electronic sigh, and Luke smiled around a mouthful of stew. Devaron's moons shone brightly in the sky—the same moons that had helped lead him to the Temple of Eedit and its secrets. Eedit's Jedi must have stood in the same spot and looked up at the same moons, back when the temple was whole and no one imagined the Jedi Order could ever fall.

"I wish I could have met them," Luke murmured. "I wish I could have learned from them."

"I beg your pardon, Master Luke?" asked Threepio, his photoreceptors like lamps in the darkness.

"I was just thinking about what it must have been like here, before the Empire. When the Jedi were the galaxy's defenders of peace and justice."

Artoo hooted mournfully, but for once Threepio thought it best to remain silent.

As he stared into the glowing heater, Luke suddenly felt very alone. His lightsaber was all that was left of his father, and possibly of the Jedi Order he'd served. He was piecing together his own training from disembodied voices, vague hunches, and equipment scavenged from ruins. It was crazy to think that he'd ever learn to command the Force or become a skilled duelist, let alone see the Jedi Order reborn. The Empire was powerful and ruthless—and it had its own enforcers who could command the Force, beings such as the terrifying, black-armored Darth Vader.

But then Luke shook his head. Destroying the Death Star had seemed impossible, too—what chance did an untrained farm boy have, alone in a trench with Vader preparing to finish him off? Yet Luke had succeeded, turning the Empire's greatest weapon into space dust. He'd done so with help from his friends, and by trusting the Force.

Luke wondered what Han and Chewbacca were doing and smiled to imagine them arguing over how to keep the *Falcon* flying this time. He thought of Princess Leia and felt his breath catch at the thought of the strong, beautiful rebel leader. He wondered what Wedge was doing and who was serving as his wingman.

He had friends. And the Force was with him.

As long as those things were true, there was reason to hope.

He held up his lightsaber, feeling the comforting weight of it in his hand.

"I never knew you, Father," he said. "But I swear I will become a Jedi. And when I do, I will honor your service and your sacrifice."

And then Luke put the saber down on the flagstones and crawled into his sleeping bag. Before he could even worry about how to face three remotes, he was asleep.

A few kilometers away, Sarco had gathered branches and leaves and built another fire. The happabores stood nearby, occasionally churning up the dirt with their snouts as they searched for roots to gnaw.

Huddled behind her tree, Farnay tried to keep her teeth from chattering as she stared through her macrobinoculars at the alien. She hadn't known what to do when the Scavenger settled down to wait for Luke—which had made her realize she hadn't known what to do when she set out after the young rebel and his guide in the first place. She'd been too worried about Luke to wait in Tikaroo for the Scavenger to return and claim he'd fallen off a cliff or been gored by a pikhron bull, or some tale that no one would ever be able to prove was a lie.

But it was clear that the Scavenger wasn't going anywhere, and she couldn't afford to spy on him any longer—she was out of food and hadn't brought supplies for an extended trip into the jungle.

Dad will know what to do, she thought, then swallowed. He'd be angry with her, of course—her comlink was filled with messages asking her where she was, which she'd acknowledged by curtly informing him she was fine.

He'd be angry with her, but he'd also know the best way to help Luke.

Farnay slipped away from the tree, wincing at each crinkle and crack of dry leaves beneath her feet. She shushed her pack beast—he was hungry, too—and led him in the direction of the jungle path and home.

CHAPTER 10
THE SECRET OF THE FORCE

KIVAS HEARD the incoming ship before he saw it, and knew immediately what it was—a *Sentinel*-class Imperial landing craft. There was something wrong with one of the fuel pumps—a clog, by the sound of it. It wasn't bad yet—the pilot probably hadn't noticed anything except a slight pull to one side on takeoff—but it would ground the ship within a week or two if not serviced.

Somehow I don't think they're here to get it fixed, Kivas thought.

Kivas knew he had a few minutes—Imperial ships coming to Tikaroo from the capital always followed the valley up from the south, then curled in to touch down on the landing field. He picked up his toolbox, pulled down the shutters on the hangar behind him, and locked the door. Then he strolled across the landing field and popped the access hatch on the starboard engine of a Mark V Struthimer star yacht that had landed yesterday.

The *Sentinel*'s engines were louder now. Kivas scattered a few tools beneath the star yacht, picked up his smallest hydrospanner, and reached up into the access hatch as the landing craft roared in over the trees and fired its retrorockets, touching down with a bump and a rattle of landing gear. The Imperial craft's fuel pump was in worse shape than he'd thought.

Kivas glanced over at the landing craft, then put his gloved hands back into the engine he was pretending to service. The sound of the *Sentinel*'s engines died away, and a minute later he heard the tramp of boot heels approaching. He looked over with what he hoped would seem like mild curiosity and saw an olive-green-clad officer approaching with a squad of stormtroopers behind him.

Kivas stripped off his dirty work gloves and stepped away from the star yacht.

"What can I do for you, Lieutenant?" he asked after eyeing the rank badge on the officer's uniform. Some Imperials reacted badly if you addressed them by the wrong rank.

"We're looking for a starfighter that was spotted in this area three days ago," the lieutenant said, hands behind his back. "It belongs to a suspected fugitive from Imperial justice."

"Oh?" Kivas asked. "Lots of places a starfighter might have set down around here. But we're pretty remote—odds are the pilot would have followed the river to Assarda or Ton-biri."

"And if he did another squad will find him," the lieutenant said. "This area is our responsibility. Do you have anything to report?"

Kivas saw the lieutenant's eyes lingering on the star yachts.

"As the governor knows, the only traffic we get is from hunters going into the jungle," he said carefully, hoping the officer was familiar with the governor's orders to let the hunts go on without interference. "But our customers don't typically show up in starfighters."

"Then you won't mind if we take a look in the hangar?"

"Of course not," Kivas said, fighting down a sense of dread. "But first, you should know your starboard fuel pump is clogged. It could cut out any minute. I'd be happy to fix it. As a favor to the Empire."

"How considerate. You can do so after we look in the hangar."

The lieutenant turned and indicated two of his troopers. "You two stay here."

Kivas led the officer and the other stormtroopers across the landing field to the hangar. He knew there was nothing to be done—trying to delay them further would only make things worse in the end.

At least Farnay was safe. Kivas had been angry to discover their pack beast gone, and frightened when he realized his daughter had followed Sarco into the jungle. Worry had woken him before dawn that morning, and he'd headed to the landing field because he'd known he wouldn't be able to get back to sleep. But now he found himself relieved that his daughter had made the choice she did. It was a foolish decision, but Farnay knew the jungle, and at least her rash act had taken her far from Tikaroo.

He unlocked the hangar, raised the shutters with a rattle, and turned on the overhead lights. The officer looked at the Y-wing and raised an eyebrow.

"And you said you had nothing to report," he said.

"I'm just trying to make a living," Kivas stammered. "I wanted the starfighter as salvage."

"I see. And where did it come from?"

Kivas paused, and the officer put his hands on his hips.

"The truth, please," he said. "It would be a shame to have to take you in for interrogation."

"The owner isn't here," Kivas said. "He went into the woods and hasn't returned."

And probably won't, Kivas thought, looking guiltily at the Y-wing.

"Into the jungle? Did he go alone?"

"No. Two droids were with him. And he had a guide."

"And where is this guide?"

"I don't know."

The officer raised an eyebrow.

"I really don't. I spend most of my time here, not in town. Last I knew, the guide hadn't come back, either."

The two troopers who'd been left to guard the landing field strode into the hangar, holding someone between them by the upper arms.

Kivas tried to keep his face expressionless.

"I'm sorry, Dad," Farnay said.

The Imperial lieutenant looked from the frightened girl to Kivas.

"Your daughter?"

Kivas nodded grimly.

"Was she the pilot's guide?"

Farnay looked at him in surprise, still struggling in the troopers' grip.

"No," Kivas said. "It wasn't her."

The officer studied Farnay for a long moment.

"But you know where the pilot went, don't you?" he asked her.

Farnay's eyes jumped beseechingly to her father. But the lieutenant's gaze had turned his way, too.

"You better tell them," Kivas told his daughter.

"Dad, no!"

"Your father's a wise man," the officer said. "I'd listen to him."

"Not unless these two Ferijian apes let go of me," Farnay said, kicking at one of the stormtroopers.

The officer nodded at his men, who relaxed their grip. Farnay stood for a moment with her eyes downcast, rubbing each arm in turn.

"They went to Eedit," she muttered.

"The old temple?" the officer asked, eyebrows raised. "Are you sure? There's been no intrusion alarm."

"I'm sure."

"Very well," the officer said. "We can depart after I verify your story in town—and after you fix the fuel pump you're so concerned about. But we could use a guide ourselves. This young lady will do nicely."

"She's answered your questions," Kivas objected. "Leave her alone."

"If she does her duty no harm will come to her. I find using someone local encourages good behavior."

The lieutenant's eyes lingered on the Y-wing. Then he turned to Kivas with a smile.

"And as loyal Imperial citizens, I'm sure you welcome the chance to help the Empire maintain peace and order," he said.

———

The sun was burning off the dew, the birds were singing, and the pikhrons were nibbling at fruit in the branches of the trees.

Time to get to work, Luke thought.

He had dreamt all night of lightsaber combat, of repositioning his feet, bending his knees, and angling his blade according to each of the four defensive postures, then switching to downward slashes and side cuts when attacking. His shoulders and arms hurt, but it was a good ache, the kind that followed hard work.

"I detest those dreadful remotes," Threepio said as he followed Artoo out of the way. "I swear they enjoy inflicting pain."

The previous morning Luke might have agreed with Threepio. Now, he just approached the pillar and ignited his saber. The remotes rose from their compartment as soon as he assumed the ready position, spiraling around each other and then spreading out to flank him.

The one on the right darted in, and Luke snapped his saber to stop its laser bolt, then whipped the blade back to the left, deflecting another. Then he stepped forward, forcing the remote in the center to give way before it could fire.

"Master Luke! You're doing it!" Threepio called.

Luke grinned—and one of the remotes dove and shot him in the thigh. Artoo beeped his concern.

"How is it *my* fault?" Threepio asked Artoo. "Everyone needs a little encouragement."

Luke's leg felt like it was asleep. He rubbed the circulation back into it, grimacing, and turned to face the remotes again, willing the Force to give him the speed and stamina he needed to fight three enemies at once.

Left and right, up and down, forward and back. Luke's saber was a whirling disc of energy, scattering laser bolts like rain. He could hear his heart hammering in his chest, his breath loud in his ears.

One of the remotes used another for cover, slipping a beam of energy through Luke's defenses and catching him in the shoulder. He bent over, breathing hard.

That was a scoot and shoot, he thought. *Wedge would be proud.*

"How long since the last time I was hit?" he asked Threepio.

"Thirty-two minutes and twenty-four seconds."

Luke nodded. He waited a moment, breathing hard, then got back in the ready position. The remotes swarmed him and he lifted the lightsaber, scattering their bolts and dancing across the courtyard. He skirted the pits and splashed through the pool left by the spring bubbling up through the broken fountain, while the birds zipped from tree to tree and the pikhrons watched quietly.

A laser beam caught him in the calf and he shouted in surprise, the lightsaber spinning out of his hands and shutting off in the air. He plucked it out of the grass with a grimace.

"How long that time?"

"Fourteen minutes and two seconds," Threepio said.

Luke's hair was dark with sweat. He ignited the lightsaber, noticing to his dismay that his hands were shaking.

Six minutes and thirty-three seconds later two remotes got him at once, catching him in the back of the thigh.

Luke reminded himself to push the anger and anxiety out of his mind, taking several calming breaths. His palms were sweaty where they gripped his father's lightsaber. He felt the negative emotions draining away and nodded. But he still felt tired—arms heavy, feet sluggish, his eyes and ears a beat behind the movements of the remotes as they waited for him to resume the exercise.

He lasted less than two minutes before one of the remotes got him in the side of the head, making his ears ring.

Then he was hit after forty-two seconds.

And then after eight.

Luke hurled his lightsaber aside, gasping for breath. Artoo whistled urgently.

"I quite agree with Artoo," Threepio said. "Master Luke, you must rest. You're only human, after all."

Luke flopped down on the grassy flagstones, his chest rising and falling as the remotes retreated to wait inside the pillar.

"I haven't done enough," he said raggedly. "Haven't completed the exercise."

"Surely a rest isn't against the rules."

"No, probably not," Luke gasped.

He sat in the grass until he was no longer short of breath and the sweat had stopped running down his face. He got to his feet and walked slowly to where his lightsaber lay, bending to pick it up. His legs ached, and the ancient weapon felt heavy in his hand.

"Master Luke, are you quite sure you're recovered?" Threepio asked. "I'd hate to see you damaged."

"I'm fine," Luke said, though he was pretty sure that wasn't true.

"Next you'll tell me you have to fight again without being able to see," Threepio said. "If you don't mind my saying so, that seemed terribly reckless."

Luke smiled, remembering standing in the hold of the *Falcon* and trying to track the remote by the hiss of its jets, with the blast shield of Han's old bucket of a flight helmet covering his eyes. He'd thought Ben was crazy—he could barely control a lightsaber, let alone use it without being able to see. Only his loyalty to the old Jedi had kept him from protesting more vigorously in front of Han and Chewbacca.

But he'd done it. He'd stopped the remote, without being able to use his eyes. It had been his first lesson in how the Force could enhance one's senses.

Luke raised his lightsaber, and the remotes advanced immediately. He parried one strike, then another, listening for each hiss of a remote's changing direction, eyes tracking each tiny repositioning.

A laser beam caught him in the thigh.

"Twenty-six seconds, Master Luke."

I can't do this, Luke thought. *Honestly, I'd be better off blind.*

And then he realized.

The point of fighting with the blast shield covering his eyes hadn't been to enhance his other senses. It had been to give him no choice but to trust in the Force. He'd done it then—and again in the Death Star trench, when he'd shut off his targeting computer and let the Force tell him when to fire the proton torpedoes that had destroyed the battle station.

Let go, Ben's voice had said. That had been the key— the simple instruction that had saved the Alliance and his own life.

He hadn't understood his own training there at Eedit. He'd thought he'd been commanding the Force, using it to amplify his senses and speed up his reflexes. But that hadn't been it at all. When he'd succeeded, it was because he was letting the Force guide him—and when he'd failed, it was because he was trying to guide it. He'd thought that he was learning to make the Force obey his commands, but really it was the other way around.

Let go, Luke thought, breathing out.

He couldn't track three remotes at once—it was hard enough keeping up with one. And all the practice in the galaxy wouldn't help him. That wasn't the point of the exercise any more than whether or not he could see.

"Are you all right, Master Luke?" Threepio asked.

"I'm fine," Luke said. "Threepio, you're a genius."

"I like to think I'm programmed for insights," Threepio said, to which Artoo offered a disgusted blat.

Luke raised his blade to ready position, ignoring the ache in his shoulders and the sweat stinging his eyes.

The remotes streaked in. Luke couldn't say that he saw them, but the blade of his father's lightsaber was there to block their energy bolts. He couldn't say that he heard them, but he turned whenever one tried to get behind him, blocking its attack vector with his blade.

He was no longer aware of Threepio's encouragement, or Artoo's beeps. The chirping birds no longer registered in his ears, nor the chuffs and snorts of the pikhrons. He didn't notice the sweat running down his neck, or feel the growing heat of the day.

There was only the Force, its currents stretching into the past and future, and he was part of it, trusting it to take him where he needed to be. His muscles and nerves moved his arms and legs, shifting effortlessly among the four defensive postures that formed the foundation of lightsaber combat. But who was commanding those muscles and nerves?

The remotes broke off their attack and floated quietly in front of the pillar. Luke looked around the courtyard, faintly startled. The sun had passed directly overhead and was now descending from its zenith in the sky.

"How long . . . how long since I was last hit?" he asked.

"Three standard hours, eleven minutes, and forty-three seconds," Threepio said. "Perhaps you ought to rest, Master Luke. You must be perilously low on charge."

"I feel great," Luke said with a smile, wanting nothing more than to sink back into the Force and lose himself in it.

The pikhrons began to snuffle and snort, tossing their heads. The matriarch brought her front feet off the ground and slammed them down, calling urgently to the rest of the group.

"Now what's gotten into those peculiar creatures?" Threepio wondered.

"I think they sense something," Luke said. "They're acting like banthas did back home when a krayt dragon was on the hunt."

Then he could feel it, too—new ripples in the Force, advancing like waves to crash into the gentle ebb and flow of life in the glade.

He raised his lightsaber, and the remotes rose up to face him.

"No," Luke said. "We're not training now. Something else is happening."

He lowered his weapon, and the remotes backed away—which was when the laser blast knocked him off his feet.

CHAPTER 11
IMPERIAL ATTACK

THE STORMTROOPERS clambered over the rubble of the ruined outbuildings with their blasters raised.

"Oh no, I'll be captured!" yelped Threepio, throwing his hands in the air.

The pikhrons huddled together in terror, bellowing.

Luke scrambled to his feet. He glanced quickly at his gun belt, but it was on the other side of the fountain. He'd never reach it in time.

"Surrender, rebel," said the lead trooper.

"Come get me," Luke said, his feet automatically assuming the ready position as he raised his lightsaber.

The stormtrooper adjusted his rifle's controls, no doubt setting it for stun.

I can't let them capture me, Luke thought. *They'll figure out who I am and make a symbol out of me. The destroyer of the Death*

Star, brought to justice. And then many worlds that might have joined the Alliance will retreat in fear instead.

The lead trooper fired at him, blaster emitting rings of concentric blue. Luke barely intercepted them with his blade, the energy dancing along it and vanishing.

And of course if they capture me I'll be executed, Luke thought. *I'd rather avoid that, too.*

The stormtrooper paused, then nodded at his fellows. The squad began to spread out, advancing across the glade toward him.

Let the Force guide you, Luke thought. But he turned uncertainly one way and then the other as the troopers executed a flanking maneuver.

There's too many of them, shrilled the voice of doubt in his head. *Three remotes isn't anything like eight living adversaries.*

Behind the troopers came a slim man wearing the olive-green uniform of an Imperial officer, dragging along a smaller figure. It was Farnay. Their eyes met and Luke saw the anger in her gaze—anger and fear.

"Drop your weapon," the officer said, inclining his chin at the girl in his grip. "Otherwise someone could get hurt."

Luke took a step back. He was outnumbered nine to one, and the Imperials had Farnay. He sighed and held his finger over the lightsaber's activation stud.

Then a hum reached his ears, followed by a surprised beep from Artoo.

Luke risked a glance backward. Sarco was striding through the archway that led into the Temple of Eedit. He was carrying a staff whose ends were crowned with cycling purple sparks. The weapon howled and crackled in his hands, and Luke found himself thinking that this was not the Sarco he'd met in the jungle—the being crossing the courtyard radiated both confidence and malice.

"Hyperspace scout," Sarco said. "Historian. Farm boy. And yet here you are with a Jedi laser sword in your hand, like you mean to use it."

"Be quiet," the Imperial lieutenant said. "You're under arrest, both of you."

"I don't think so," Sarco replied, twisting a dial on his tool belt. Artoo let out an electronic shriek, Threepio stopped and flung his arms in the air, and the troopers clutched their helmets.

"What was that?" Luke demanded.

"Electromagnetic pulse to block their transmissions," Sarco said. "Well, Marcus? Let's see what you're capable of."

The faceless alien whirled the staff in his hands as he strode across the courtyard. The weapon let out a strange howl, purple lightning flaring from either end. One of the troopers fired at Sarco, a panicky shot that went wide, and the alien speared the trooper with his staff, sending purple energy coursing across his armor. The trooper flopped on the ground, spasming, then lay still.

The lieutenant drew his sidearm, but Farnay drove her elbow into his stomach, breaking his grip. She scrambled away from him, head down. The officer aimed his blaster at her, and Luke raced forward, lightsaber held at his waist.

A trooper fired at him—the shot was to kill, not stun—and Luke deflected the bolt into the chest of the lieutenant. The man fell forward with a strangled cry. Luke brought his lightsaber down on the trooper's helmet, then spun away from the falling soldier and blocked a shot at point-blank range, sending the laser blast back into the chest of the trooper who'd fired it.

The pikhrons broke into a run, charging over the rubble behind the troopers, seeking safety.

Sarco brought his staff down like a club on a trooper's head, then thrust the end into the fallen Imperial's breastplate. He grunted as a blaster bolt struck the middle of the staff but held on and charged the trooper who'd tried to disarm him, screaming like a Tusken in the Tatooine night.

Something told Luke to duck. He did, then smelled his hair burning. He swung around, thrusting his lightsaber up and through the armored breastplate of a trooper. He spotted Farnay crouched behind the rim of the fountain, watching the fight anxiously.

The remaining two stormtroopers were between Luke and Sarco. Sarco swung his staff forward as one trooper fired wildly. The alien's weapon hooked the soldier's blaster and ripped it out of his hands. The other trooper dropped to one knee and raised his rifle at Luke, who deflected the bolt back at him. The soldier ducked, and the reoriented bolt struck his squadmate in the back of the helmet. Then Sarco stepped over the armored body and brought his staff down on the last trooper's head.

Luke stepped back, lowering his lightsaber. It had all happened so quickly.

"I don't know why you followed me," he said to Sarco. "But I'm glad you did."

The stormtroopers had been the danger he'd sensed in the Force. But he'd defeated them—thanks to the mystical energy field, and help from his friends. His vision hadn't been completely accurate—he hadn't slipped on a flagstone, for one thing—but it had been close enough to warn him.

"Are you all right?" he called to Farnay.

She nodded, eyes wide.

Sarco turned his head in the girl's direction, then walked past Luke and shoved one of the motionless troopers into a pit blasted in the flagstones.

"What are you doing?" Luke asked.

"Making it harder for the Empire to figure out what

happened here," Sarco said, dragging another trooper over to vanish into the darkness. "Pity. Their weapons and armor would be good salvage."

Luke hesitated, but disposing of the troopers made sense. The two of them shoved the other fallen soldiers into the pits.

"Look out!" Farnay yelled.

Luke looked up to see Sarco spinning his staff slowly in one hand.

"Stay away from him!" Farnay yelled.

"What are you going to do about it, brat?" snarled Sarco. "This is no business of yours."

He cocked his head at Luke, to the left and then to the right.

"What are you, Marcus?" he asked. "I've been considering that since back in the jungle. You're no hyperspace scout, that's for sure. And you can use that sorcerer's weapon better than you let on."

Luke took a step backward, raising his lightsaber. The remotes rushed forward, thinking he meant to resume the exercise. Luke slipped on a loose flagstone, nearly falling to his knees. He looked from the flagstone to Sarco in sudden realization.

"The Force wasn't warning me about the stormtroopers," he said. "It was warning me about *you*."

"Oh no," Threepio moaned.

"The Force," Sarco said. "So you're a Jedi, then?

I don't think so. I remember them from when I was small—you don't have their skills. So what are you? What was the word the sorcerers used, before the Empire came for them? *Padawan*—that was it. So that's what you are—a learner. An apprentice. But what good's an apprentice without a master?"

Sarco skirted the edge of a pit, walking toward Luke like he had all the time in the world. Luke found his feet assuming ready position, noting with relief that the remotes had finally concluded something other than a training exercise was taking place.

"Nobody's Padawan, the last apprentice of an extinct religion," Sarco said. "Care for a duel?"

Luke felt his anger rising. Sarco had proposed the one thing he wanted most—a chance to show off his new skills and show the arrogant alien what a mistake he'd made.

He exhaled slowly, lightsaber held at his waist, as Sarco spun his staff in a blur of deadly purple.

"I should thank you, Nobody's Padawan," he said. "I've been looking for a way into this place for years—and now you've been good enough to find one for me."

"And now you know there's nothing left here for you to steal."

Sarco's vocoder erupted in amused static.

"That's where you're wrong, Nobody's Padawan. The Empire bombed the temple, but the vaults and storerooms below are intact. I've got debts to pay, and what's beneath our feet will take care of that and more. Pity you won't get to see the wealth your precious sorcerers left behind."

"The Jedi didn't stockpile wealth like that," Luke said. "The only treasures here are what's around you."

Sarco turned his chitinous mask to take in the broken statues and uprooted flagstones, then returned his scrutiny to Luke.

"Do you know what I'm going to do after I defeat you, Nobody's Padawan?" he asked. "First I'll sell whatever's left of you to the governor. Then I'll sell your fighter and melt those droids into scrap. As for your saber, it will fetch good credits from some collector. Or perhaps I'll keep it as one of my trophies."

"None of those things is going to happen," Luke said, and leapt forward, lightsaber held over his head.

CHAPTER 12
THE SCAVENGER'S STAFF

SARCO FELL BACK, and Luke's vicious downward cut bit into the flagstones, sending up sparks. The alien held his staff up to parry as Luke stalked him.

"You don't know the first thing about Jedi," Luke said. "Starting with their weapons."

Sarco raised his staff, and Luke brought the saber down, expecting the ancient weapon to cleave the Scavenger's staff in two. But the saber met resistance as Sarco's staff caught the blade and held it, sending a shock up Luke's arms. Sarco gave way, and Luke stumbled forward. Then the alien kicked the young rebel in the face, sending him sprawling.

"You ruffian!" yelled Threepio.

"This is an electrostaff, Nobody's Padawan," Sarco

said as Luke struggled to his feet, spitting out blood. "A useful tool—and one designed to kill Jedi."

Farnay looked around the courtyard in desperation. Luke hoped she wouldn't try anything foolish—the Scavenger would kill her with barely a thought.

Sarco leapt forward, the electrostaff whining with what sounded like a terrible glee. Luke got his lightsaber up and knocked the weapon aside, but Sarco followed him, sweeping at his stomach with the staff. Luke turned aside as Sarco charged and aimed a slash at the alien's back—but Sarco had anticipated the attack and batted Luke's blade away, leaping over a crater in the glade and turning to regard his opponent.

"It's a pity," he said. "In a couple of years you might have passed for a Jedi. But now you're just a boy with a blade you're not worthy of. A dreamer, Marcus. Pretending to be something you're not."

"The Force is with me," Luke said. "That's more than you'll ever have."

He carved a figure eight in the air in front of him, telling himself to let the Force guide his hand. Sarco stepped back, then tried to dodge around Luke's defenses. Quicker than thought, Luke's lightsaber was there to meet the electrostaff, pushing Sarco back.

The alien grunted and spun away from Luke's blade, tumbling forward and then leaping at Luke's unprotected back, electrostaff wailing. But the blow never landed—and then the brilliant blue blade was slashing at Sarco's head. He caught the blade on his staff and scrambled aside, the bristles on his arms rising and falling as if they were breathing hard.

"Not bad, Nobody's Padawan," he said. "Your teacher would praise you. If you had a teacher."

Again Sarco attacked, electrostaff thrust in front of him like a spear. Luke knocked the tip aside, but Sarco's charge was too powerful to deflect. He ducked, and Sarco stumbled past, Luke's lightsaber flashing behind him and nicking the back of the alien's leg.

Sarco grunted, one chitinous hand going to the cut on his thigh. His cilia flailed back and forth, and the hairs on his arms spasmed.

Farnay scrambled to Artoo's side. He beeped at her in dismay.

"No more games, boy," Sarco said, touching a button on the control box that sat on his chest. Motors squealed and a hidden shield emerged from inside his helmet, covering his chitinous face. He opened a pouch on his tool belt and extracted a small black sphere.

"Master Luke, look out!" Threepio yelped as Sarco tossed the object at Luke—some kind of grenade, he thought.

Luke watched it calmly, his lightsaber already moving to intercept it. Interrupting the grenade's trajectory would be easy enough.

But that wasn't the Scavenger's plan.

The grenade detonated at the apex of its flight, a meter before Luke would have sliced it in two.

A blinding flash of light and a thunderclap of noise filled the courtyard. The concussion knocked Luke backward into the overflow from the fountain. He staggered to his feet, lightsaber in hand, blood running from his nose.

Luke blinked furiously, then stared straight ahead.

Sarco put a finger to his chest, and his face shield contracted back into his helmet. He took two steps to the right, spinning his staff. Luke kept staring in the same direction, his knees shaking.

"Hey!" Sarco called. "Nobody's Padawan!"

Luke didn't react to the words. He held the lightsaber in front of him, blinking desperately, wiping his bloody nose on his sleeve with an uncertain, jittery movement. He staggered to the left, then to the right, then fell to his knees, struggling to lift his head.

"You've blinded him!" Threepio shrieked. "He can't see or hear! It isn't a fair fight!"

"Who said it would be?" Sarco asked the droid. "Be quiet and maybe I'll sell you and your little friend instead of pulling you apart."

Luke scrambled to his feet, swinging his lightsaber wildly, then crashed to the ground again.

"Such feeble senses—so easily disabled," Sarco said.

Static coughed out of the alien's vocoder. He walked slowly around the fallen Jedi, raising his deadly electrostaff as if he meant to ram it into Luke's back. He held it a few centimeters from Luke, then drew it away, turning in the direction of Farnay and the droids.

"Good news—I've decided not to sell your master to the Empire," he said. "I'm going to keep him as one of my own trophies instead. I can't wait to hear him scream."

"Oh no," Threepio said. "My poor master."

Sarco once again brought the staff to within a few centimeters of the back of Luke's head, prompting a gasp from Farnay and an electronic squeal from Artoo.

"I can't bear to watch," Threepio said.

Stones rattled nearby. Threepio looked up and saw the pikhron matriarch scrambling back into the glade over the pile of rubble, followed by the other beasts. The matriarch stared at the alien and the stricken rebel and snorted, pawing at the grass.

"Even better," Sarco said. "When I'm done with your master I'll take these foolish beasts' hides and teeth."

The Scavenger walked around to face Luke. The young rebel was on his knees, blinking furiously. He waved his lightsaber weakly in front of him, and Sarco took a half step back, the movement relaxed and casual.

"You'll never see it coming," Sarco purred, raising the electrostaff like a club.

A laser bolt zipped past the alien's head. He spun away, electrostaff held in front of him. Then he turned, the bristles on his arms twitching.

"Get away from him, Scavenger," Farnay said, holding Luke's blaster pistol in front of her.

The bristles on Sarco's arms fluttered.

"Foolish brat," he said, walking around Luke toward the girl. "You've interfered with me for the last time."

"Stop," Farnay said. "Put down your weapon or I'll shoot you."

Sarco strode forward, electrostaff held to one side. He spun it idly in his hand.

"You mean this weapon?" he asked.

"Not another step," Farnay said, trying to hold Luke's pistol steady. "I mean it."

Sarco broke into a run. Farnay fired at him, one shot nearly clipping his shoulder, before he leveled her with a forearm. Her gun went flying, and a moment later Sarco had slapped binders on her wrists, behind her back. He threw her to the ground and held the electrostaff near her throat.

"Let her alone, you brute!" Threepio yelped.

"Five seconds' contact and your heart will stop,"

Sarco told Farnay, cilia quivering eagerly. "Shall I do it here? Or take you back to Tikaroo so your worthless father can watch?"

"Leave . . . leave her alone."

The voice was weak and came from some distance behind Sarco. He pulled his staff back from Farnay's throat. Luke had gotten to his feet and was holding his saber in front of him. But the young rebel was still facing the wrong way, disoriented.

Static bubbled out of Sarco's vocoder. He picked up Luke's blaster and tucked it into his belt.

"You're a determined one, Marcus," he said. "But it's a little too late for that Force of yours. Enough foolishness—time to end this."

He gave Farnay a contemptuous kick and strode across the courtyard, electrostaff aimed at Luke's back.

CHAPTER 13

MY ALLY IS THE FORCE

WHEN THE GRENADE went off, Luke found himself in darkness, with no sound except the ringing in his ears. He got to his feet, feeling the familiar weight of his father's lightsaber in his hand. But he could barely stand. He tried to call on the Force, begging it to keep him on his feet, but his senses were clouded by fear and pain.

He could sense Sarco somewhere nearby—but where he couldn't say. One moment it felt like he was in front of Luke, the next behind. Luke staggered and fell to his knees, his heartbeat hammering in his head. All he wanted to do was lie down and sleep—sleep for ages and ages.

If you go to sleep you'll never wake up, he told himself. *Or if you do, you'll wish you never had.*

He reached out with the Force. He could feel the

malignant throb of Sarco, like a darker stain on the void around him. He could feel the birds and insects of the glade—they'd retreated to a safe distance, their wariness pulsing in the Force. He could feel the agitated presence of the pikhrons.

And he could feel Farnay, her energy spiky and jagged with terror.

He got shakily to his feet again, gasping for Sarco to leave the girl alone. He couldn't hear his own voice.

Help me, Ben Kenobi, he thought. *Somebody help me.*

He could feel Sarco nearby, but he didn't know where. Luke raised his lightsaber to the ready position. He knew it was a useless gesture, but it was all he could do.

"Let go, Luke," said Ben's voice. "Your eyes and ears can deceive you. But the Force is all-seeing."

Farnay began to scream when Sarco got within a meter of Luke's unprotected back. The pikhrons looked up, jerking their heads up and down as they pawed at the grass.

Sarco twirled his electrostaff in lazy contemplation. Thrusting the weapon into the boy's spine would knock him unconscious for several hours, and it would be a day or more before he could use his legs. By then it would be far too late for him. He'd take the girl and the droids back into the jungle with him, then wait for the Empire to search for its missing squad. When they were gone, he'd have all the time he needed to loot the temple.

Luke began to swing his lightsaber wildly, a desperate defense against an enemy who wasn't there. Standing safely behind him, Sarco spun his staff lazily.

"Monster," Farnay spat, yanking futilely at her binders.

Sarco had had enough. He raised his staff, attention fixed on the motionless rebel's unprotected back, on the perfect spot to drive his weapon home.

The Scavenger didn't bother to react when the blinded boy slashed uselessly at the empty air to his left. But then Luke continued the movement, repositioning his feet perfectly as he spun around. The lightsaber moved at incredible speed with all of Luke's weight behind it, its path a perfect arc that remained smooth and graceful even as the blue-white blade ripped through Sarco's chest.

The bristles on Sarco's arms stood straight out and he screeched. His fingers opened, and the electrostaff fell from them, setting the grass afire.

The alien's hand groped at his chest. Luke's blade had slashed through the control box, leaving a ragged wound in Sarco's chest. One tube flapped freely, a pale green fluid gushing from it. The smell—thick and nauseatingly sweet—reached Luke's nose.

Sarco staggered a step to the right, then tottered two steps to the left. Luke stood facing him, eyes unseeing, braced for another attack.

Sarco drew Luke's pistol, aiming it between the rebel's eyes. The gun wavered in the Scavenger's hand as he fought to concentrate, distracted by a sudden hammering sound nearby.

The pikhrons were charging across the glen, trumpeting in fury.

The great beasts' massive sides passed within a few centimeters of Luke as he stood in the glade. He didn't move—the Force told him he was safe, just as it had guided his hand at the moment of gravest peril.

Sarco fired at the onrushing pikhrons, but the volley of shots merely bounced off the matriarch's thick hide. He backed up—and his foot found empty air. He hung for a moment on the lip of one of the pits gouged in the courtyard, arms flailing in a desperate attempt to regain his balance. But it was too late. The Scavenger's last scream lingered behind him as he fell into darkness.

Water.

Luke could feel water—cool, soothing water. It was on his forehead, and his cheeks, and then his chin.

He gasped, opening his eyes to look into the face

of Farnay, who was sponging his forehead with a wet cloth.

"You're alive," she said.

For a moment Luke wondered if that was true. He had spots in his vision, the blood was hammering in his ears, and he felt like his head was going to split in two. But it was true—he was alive.

Binders hung from Farnay's wrists, the link broken by a cutting torch. Behind the Devaronian girl he could see Threepio and Artoo staring down at him in concern. Around the four of them the pikhrons stood in a protective ring.

"How . . . how did you get here?" Luke managed.

"I followed you and the Scavenger," Farnay said. "He stayed to wait for you. I didn't know what to do, so I went home—just in time to get caught by the stormtroopers. I didn't have any choice, Luke—they would have hurt my dad if I hadn't come with them. Oh, I messed everything up, didn't I?"

"Messed everything up? You saved my life."

"You did that yourself," Farnay said with a small smile. "I didn't know the Scavenger had followed you into the cave."

"I guess he wanted the bounty on me," Luke said.

"He wanted you for his collection," Farnay said, and Luke thought back to the gloomy clearing and the half-buried bones. "As well as whatever he could steal from the temple. The Empire must be trying to contact the troopers by now—they'll be overdue. Can you stand?"

"I'll crawl if I have to," Luke said, getting shakily to his feet with Threepio and Farnay's help and clipping his lightsaber to his belt.

"I thought you were dead," Farnay said. "How did you do that?"

Luke smiled.

"The Force showed me my enemy. As well as my friends."

He stretched his hand out to the pikhron matriarch, stroking her scaly muzzle. She closed her eyes and sighed, and Luke bowed his head to her, then to the rest of the creatures standing around them.

"Go on now," Luke said gently. "You don't want to be here when the Empire comes back."

The matriarch snorted and began to make her way toward the pile of rubble, the rest of her clan falling in line behind her. One by one the great beasts climbed over the debris and disappeared.

Artoo whistled urgently.

"Master Luke, Artoo says he's detecting the sound of ion engines," Threepio said.

"We'd better go," Luke said.

Sarco's electrostaff lay in the grass, deactivated. At

either end a circle of grass was burnt black. Luke bent and picked up the weapon, eyeing it with distaste, then walked cautiously to the edge of the pit and peered into it.

He saw nothing but darkness. But there was a faint tickle in the back of his brain, like an unpleasant smell one could just detect. And he knew the Scavenger was alive.

Let him rot then, Luke thought. *Down there with the imaginary treasure he wanted so badly.*

He threw the electrostaff into the pit. He heard the rattle of its fall, then silence.

TIE fighters shrieked somewhere overhead. Luke nodded to Farnay, and they hurried out of the courtyard as fast as Luke's still shaky legs could carry him, the droids trailing behind. The great hall was lit with shafts of late-afternoon sun, casting the shapes of the Jedi statues in shadow on the far wall. The shadows looked whole, Luke thought.

"Just one more moment," Luke said as they reached the tunnel leading back to the cave and the river valley.

He knelt in the middle of the hall, resting his hand atop the Jedi's massive stone one.

"The Force brought me here," he said quietly. "And what I learned here saved me."

He swallowed, then continued. "I will become a Jedi. I will rebuild the Order. And one day I will come here again. I swear it on the memory of Obi-Wan Kenobi. And my father. And all the Jedi who walked these halls."

He got to his feet. The sun was almost at the horizon. It was time to go.

EPILOGUE

JESSIKA PAVA'S COMLINK chimed for the third time in the previous five minutes.

"Hold on a sec, Threepio," she said with a scowl, activating the device. "Yes? It's Pava. What's that? All right—I'm on my way. Be there in a minute."

She shut off her comlink and shrugged at Threepio. "Afraid I'm needed in the command center."

"I understand, Blue Three."

She smiled. "Call me Jessika. Before I go, I want to hear how you got off Devaron. The Empire found Skywalker's Y-wing, after all. So how did you get away?"

"That *is* a tale," Threepio said. "When we returned to Tikaroo—"

"I'm afraid I only have time for the short version, Threepio. The *very* short version."

"Oh," Threepio said, sounding disappointed. "Well,

Miss Pava, Master Luke reclaimed his starfighter—which had been repaired quite capably by Kivas, I must say. On the way to space he dropped several bombs at the base of the spire, cutting off the paths into the jungle. I'm pleased to say that meant the end of those dreadful hunts."

"And the alien? The one they called the Scavenger?"

"Just recalling that awful creature puts me at risk of a short circuit," Threepio said. "Master Luke claimed he was alive. My sensors detected no trace of him, but he was quite insistent."

Jessika's comlink was chiming again.

"Stang! I said in a minute, didn't I?"

"You did," Threepio said. "And it has been one minute and two seconds exactly."

"Right. I have to go. But . . . just tell me about Farnay. Did you ever see her again?"

"Oh, yes," Threepio said. "Artoo and I were delighted to be reacquainted with Farnay when Master Luke kept his promise and returned to Devaron. She'd grown into quite a capable young woman. It would be my pleasure to tell you that story, Miss Pava. But there goes your comlink again, the beastly thing. So I suppose that tale will have to wait. . . ."